DEEP BLUE

INDUSTRIAL ESPIONAGE, IBM AND THE CIA

DEEP BLUE

INDUSTRIAL ESPIONAGE, IBM AND THE CIA

Recollections of a Corporate Spy

DON FRANCK

NEXT CENTURY
PUBLISHING

DEEP BLUE
INDUSTRIAL ESPIONAGE, IBM AND THE CIA

Published by Next Century Publishing
Las Vegas, Nevada
www.NextCenturyPublishing.com

ISBN: 978-1-68102-287-1

Printed in the United States of America

This book is dedicated to my many friends who encouraged me to write it, and to my children, grandchildren, step-children and step-grandchildren who have supported and helped me over the years.

It is also dedicated to the US military and to the very capable people of the CIA. These patriotic associates were of terrific support to me, to our country and to the democracy we cherish in the face of today's challenges by foreign ideologies.

ACKNOWLEDGMENTS

IBM

Within IBM, I had many supporters who enabled me to accomplish my assignment over a twenty-year period. Before Steve Jobs, before Bill Gates, we were truly the "Mad Men" of the computer industry.

Ray Rinne – Ray was my manager at IBM for several years. His first assignment to me for competitive electronics packaging analysis started in IBM Endicott in the fall of 1966, after he was asked by Tom Watson Jr. what we knew about the Control Data 6600 technology. This was during the highlight of the IBM "Bet Your Company" effort on the Solid Logic Technology Program and the 360 Commercial Computer Program spearheaded by Erich Bloch and T. Vincent Learson. Later on, Ray was assigned to East Fishkill, New York, in the semiconductor packaging area, and even though I was still in Endicott, he asked me to provide competitive packaging analysis for the ceramic technology used in the SLT Program. After Ray retired from IBM as a successful senior executive at East Fishkill, he became an executive with the DuPont Company and subsequently arranged for me to accept a four-year consulting assignment with DuPont after I retired from IBM in 1987.

Pat Toole – Pat Toole originally was a manufacturing manager in the Endicott Electronic Packaging Area. His personal support, promotion, and guidance for many years was most beneficial to me personally. Later, Pat became general manager of IBM Endicott, where IBM originally started, and after that he became one of the most senior corporate executives at IBM Armonk. For my competitive analysis work, I was promoted to senior engineer with Pat's support.

John Keffer – John was most helpful to me personally during my career and promotions within IBM. He encouraged and supported me in my proposals advocating that a permanent competitive analysis person to be located in Japan, and he endorsed the concept advanced to Ted Papes, who was a senior vice president of IBM.

Dick Immershein – Dick was head of Domestic Commercial Analysis at IBM Armonk for the Systems and Product Marketing and Sales Area. John Goellar had an equivalent job for IBM World Trade. Dick personally arranged for many senior presentations and exposures by me to the highest levels within IBM Armonk, including the research division under Dr. Gomory and to other major executives such as John Opel, president of IBM; Gil Jones, president of the IBM World Trade Corporation; and Nick Katzenbach, legal counsel for IBM and ex-Attorney General in the Kennedy administration. This exposure also included presentations to members of the corporate Management Review Committee and the corporate Engineering Programming and Technology Committee (EPTC).

Dr. Jack Bertram – Prior to his untimely death while at IBM, Jack personally asked me to present regular updates of the competitive technology work I was doing. He also arranged for me to present to the very senior EPTC and the Corporate Technology Committee (CTC) members. Jack was one of the few people at IBM who understood systems design, software, and also technology.

Bob Evans – Bob was originally a senior systems manager at IBM Endicott and later on became one of the senior executives at IBM Armonk. He personally arranged for me to present to the EPTC at IBM Armonk.

Jack Kuehler – A former IBM president, member of the board of directors, and director of the Corporate Management Board, Jack was an electrical engineer and very knowledgeable in all the technologies. He was most supportive of my competitive analysis activities.

Ted Papes – After a technology alert based on a report I completed relating to displays seen at Hitachi and other booths at the Fall Joint Computer Conference in 1970, I was made part of a three-person on-site evaluation trip to Japan, headed by N. Mii, a IBM senior executive located in Japan. After the trip, Bob Avgherinos and I proposed to Ted Papes, at his request, that a corporate wide Competitive Technology Analysis

Council (CAC) be established to cover worldwide areas of many computer technologies such as for memory, logic, and electronic packaging across the world, specifically including Japan and Europe. I co-wrote the letter with Bob Avgherinos that Ted Papes signed, proposing such a committee to John Opel, president of IBM. Subsequently, the committee was formed and John Mangini was assigned from IBM Corporate to chair the committee. Over many years, Ted Papes was most encouraging and helpful to me personally regarding my exposure to the IBM executives at the highest levels of IBM.

John Mangini – John was appointed chairman of the first CAC. He and I traveled to many places around the world together as first members of the CAC. John arranged for the selection of H. B. Okamoto from IBM Japan to be trained in the United States and assigned to cover the Far East for our CAC.

H. B. Okamoto – After his selection for the CAC, we subsequently arranged for H. B. to be trained at several technology locations, including Endicott for electronic packaging; East Fishkill for logic; and Burlington for memory. H. B. and I and John Mangini became close friends.

Dr. Ed Davis – Ed Davis was a senior executive in the SLT Program, working for Erich Bloch. He was an early supporter of my activities and was very encouraging and complimentary to me personally.

Carl Conti and Bob McFadden – Both were executives at IBM Endicott before going on to higher levels at IBM Corporate. They were most helpful to my competitive analysis activities and IBM career.

Tom Dougherty – Tom was one of the senior Endicott lab directors who was most helpful to me personally. He arranged to get me assigned to the Endicott lab just before my retirement, and enabled me to select my own projects before I retired. One project was a study related to the advantages and disadvantages of using CMOS versus bipolar circuits for a simulated cost/performance systems technology. Both Bill Virun and John Sents were part of Tom's group, and they were quite supportive to me in this study and activity.

Hap Fisher – Hap was the manager of the Direct Access Storage Devices (DASD) competitive analysis group located in San Jose,

California. He was most instrumental in giving detailed and competent analysis of the competitive hardware he purchased and tested in his lab, and I was privileged to assist his group upon request for Competitive Electronic Packaging.

Additional – There are so many other very capable people such as George Werbizky, Dr. Don Seraphim, and Karl Hermann, who I have not mentioned above but were very helpful to me personally over the years. This includes other people I worked with and for. Some of those who I worked with or assisted me at times were Evan Davidson, Basil Harrison, Bill Reiner, and Ed Moshier from IBM East Fishkill; Jay Greenman and Ed Boerger from IBM Burlington; and Mike Flanagan, Ed Kellerman, John Simek, Ted Nickel, and Dick Moyer from IBM Endicott. Also, I'd like to acknowledge Werner Strahle from the Boeblingen, Germany lab. I apologize if I may have missed anyone.

I would be remiss in not mentioning some of my non-IBM contacts such as Jack Balde (Bell Labs), Wulf Knausenberger (AT&T), and Dan Amey (Univac). These associates and friends were important to me in many ways over the years.

Dovatron and Dover Technologies

After an exciting and rewarding career with Dovatron, I retired in June 1995. I want to thank John Pomeroy for his advice and support, as well as Ron Budacz for the seven years I spent working for him. Other people I worked with who come to mind are Carl Vertuca, who became the CFO of Dovatron after the public offering; Rich Kenehan, who was controller; and Dermott O'Flanagan, who ran the Cork operation initially.

In addition, with some of my contacts, I was able to help arrange for Morgan Stanley, via Roger Lavoie, to be part of the three investment bank groups that took Dovatron public, along with Needham and Smith Barney. I attended the tombstone celebration party at the successful closing held in New York City.

One person I should mention is Ron Snyder, who also reported to Ron Budacz and who originally ran Cencorp, a division of Dovatron located in the Boulder, Colorado area. Ron was a real entrepreneur, and he eventually became an executive of the Flextronics Corporation who later bought Dovatron for a very hefty price, with great benefit to the shareholders and personally to Ron Budacz. Ron Snyder, Ron Budacz, and I traveled to Japan on company business several times. Later on Ron Snyder became the president of the company that designed and built Crocs shoes, becoming a multimillionaire on that investment alone.

I am also indebted to Liz Corveleyn, who was a motivating influence of encouragement as well as an avid reader of my book and who made many positive and valuable suggestions. There were others who also assisted at times, such as David Poyer, Todd Keister, Linda Exman, Suzanne Bruetsch, Joanne Dunlop, Fay Cafferty, and Leigh Rozlog. I also must credit Curtis Peebles' book *The Moby Dick Project: Reconnaissance Balloons over Russia* (1991) and Paul Carroll's *Big Blues: The Unmaking of IBM* (1993) as helpful sources in preparing this memoir, as well as many Google searches.

TABLE OF CONTENTS

DEEP BLUE

INDUSTRIAL ESPIONAGE, IBM AND THE CIA

AUTHOR'S NOTE

My thirty-one years with the IBM Corporation were the most interesting I could have ever envisioned. While I was there, my major responsibilities involved competitive technology analysis or, more plainly, corporate espionage. My position gave me personal exposure to the highest levels within IBM, including presidents of worldwide divisions, members of the board of directors, and the president of IBM. The analysis and guidance about IBM competitors that I provided to IBM executives for over twenty years required gathering, analyzing, and forecasting electronic trends of competitive computer technology in the world of commercial computer development.

For me, this was a unique, rewarding, and exciting assignment. The results of this work enabled IBM, and the United States, to become, and remain for many years, the leading and dominant computer business enterprise in the world, even in the face of extremely competent competitors such as CDC, RCA, Univac, Siemens, Fujitsu, NEC, Burroughs, Amdahl, Hitachi, DEC, Data General, and many others.

Prior to my IBM experience, I was directly involved in a successful major U.S. Air Force intelligence effort to take high-altitude photos of the Soviet Union before the U2. Both during and after IBM, I was directly involved in an association with the Central Intelligence Agency (CIA), including one project to evaluate and forecast Russian computer capability. Another project involved determining nuclear status and capability in Libya while Muammar Gaddafi was in power, and yet another was associated with activities in South East Asia.

This book describes the methods I developed and used, my worldwide exposure both inside and outside that enabled my IBM assignments to be completed, and the results that were valuable to the CIA and the United States, with regard to security.

PROLOGUE

The World as It Was

In 1953 the world was a different place. For many, the devastation wrought by World War II was fading into memory. But the challenges of communist expansion were evident and active in the Korean Peninsula. The United States draft was in place, and we were fighting a war under the United Nations auspices.

I was not enrolled in college, so deferment from the draft wasn't available. I moved to Washington DC to delay the situation until I could get into college. Meanwhile, I worked as a delivery truck driver, as an auto parts salesman at Creel Brothers, and as a woman's Real Silk Hosiery and lingerie door-to-door salesman in the Navy Base area in DC. But the draft board was very persistent. It became obvious I was going to be drafted into the U.S. Army. Instead, I joined the U.S. Air Force in March 1953, not realizing that many in the air force were also stationed near the action in Korea. For a young man who wanted to keep his options open, luck seemed to be on my side.

Based on my air force test battery results, I was sent to the USAF's electronics school in Scott Field, Illinois, for a year during my enlistment; the training I received would prove intensive and valuable to me later on. Then, lo and behold, my electronics graduating class was sent to Korea. What a surprise that was. Fortunately for me, I had qualified for pilot training, which would lead to a commission as a second lieutenant. I was sent to Fort Bragg, North Carolina, to await a pilot training class assignment. To my relief, the Korean War ended by July of that same year.

I completed my pre flight training at Lackland AFB in San Antonio, Texas. I was then assigned to Malden AFB Missouri for primary pilot training where I soloed. However I eventually lost interest in being a pilot due to the number of years I would need to remain in the air force after completing pilot training and receiving a commission as a second lieutenant. I was looking forward to the end of my tour, hoping to go on to college and study electrical engineering, so I returned to the ranks to await discharge.

Then an opportunity opened up that would change my life forever. I was asked to join a special project under the U.S. Air Force Headquarters Command in Washington, D.C. It was led by USAF Chief of Staff Nathan Twining, who many may know from his association with the famed Roswell, New Mexico, alien incident; General Curtis Lemay; and Secretary of State John Foster Dulles (under President Dwight D. Eisenhower).

Called Project Grand Union, its cover was the International Geophysical Year (IGY). It ran from July 1957 to December 1958, and the initiative was designed to mark an end to the interruption of the exchange of scientific information between the East and West that occurred during the Cold War. Sixty-seven countries participated in IGY projects, which encompassed a variety of earth sciences, and both the United States and the Soviet Union launched artificial satellites during that period. However, Project Grand Union was the cover for our real purpose.

Along with others, I was selected and sent to Lowry Air Force Base in Colorado for training. The Korean War had ended, but the Cold War was in full swing. All I initially knew was that the assignment was a very high-security project. I didn't discover for months that its purpose was to use high-altitude weather balloons to clandestinely photograph the Soviet Union, which had reportedly moved all its industry behind the Ural Mountains during World War II.

I was just twenty-two years old at the time, and little did I know it, but I was about to become a spy.

CHAPTER 1

The Right Place at the Right Time

Looking back, there was nothing in my own or my family's history that could have prepared me for such a career choice. I was born at White Plains Hospital on October 22, 1933. My mother was from an Irish Catholic family and my dad was of German Lutheran heritage. My paternal grandfather, Carl Franck, came from a little town in Langmeil, Germany, which I had the opportunity to visit many years later. He immigrated to the United States at the age of sixteen to escape being conscripted into the Franco-Prussian War, which had claimed the lives of two of his cousins.

My grandfather was a tailor by trade and readily found work in New York City. Eventually, as a very successful American businessman, he bought forty acres in Scarsdale, New York, where I grew up and where four generations of our family eventually lived over the years. In those days, the community was strong and close-knit, and despite the hardships suffered by so many with the advent of World War II, we were fortunate and secure.

My brother Carl was a U.S. Army paratrooper and was also in the American 3rd Army during World War II. I was told that he was in or near our grandfather's Langmeil birthplace during his tour and had lunch with a cousin, who was in the German Army at the time, while he was there.

My other brother, Bob, attended Kings Point and became a marine engineer. During the war, he served as a chief engineer on a tanker delivering fuel oil to England while evading German submarine wolf packs. He recounted pulling into the Azores, which was neutral during

World War II, and finding German subs and their crews also on shore. His challenge was to avoid the German subs when he left Portuguese waters. Like everyone in those days, we considered the men and women who fought in World War I, World War II, and Korea our heroes, and we strongly supported them.

I attended Edgemont and Scarsdale High Schools, graduating in 1952, during the draft and Korean War. I was not a great student except in science and math, subjects I found interesting, and I was certainly an underachiever. I wasn't sure just what I wanted to do after graduation. Despite encouragement of both family and friends, I wasn't keen on going to college, and while I didn't object to the military, I wanted to choose my branch of service. In a way, I was ahead of my time. If I'd been born just ten years later, I might have been among those who "tuned in, turned on, and dropped out."

But it wasn't to be. Despite my resistance to the more conventional options available, sometimes life has a way of putting you in the right place at the right time. And so, in the space of just a few years, I went from being an unfocused underachiever to being a well-trained operative on my first top-secret mission.

CHAPTER 2

My First Mission – Project Grand Union

After intensive technical training on Project Grand Union in Colorado, armed guards put my colleagues and I on what appeared to be an 1850s-era train. This was to prevent our exposure to any outside contacts until we arrived at our destination. Days later, we were taken off the train at the Brooklyn shipyards, guided by more armed guards, and put on the MSTS Goethals, an old liberty ship from World War II, with all our equipment.

It would be easy to romanticize that first mission, or say I was filled with a sense of excitement or danger, but that wasn't the case. Truthfully, most of us had no real idea of the project's purpose at that time and wouldn't find out for months. Until then, we were more like a piece of a puzzle or cogs in a machine. We each had training for specific technical tasks, and I had the sense we were unique and hard to replace.

Our trip to England took place during the worst North Atlantic storms imaginable. The waves crashed higher than the ship's bow. We were cold, miserable, and occasionally seasick, and when we landed at Southampton, England, we still did not know our real mission.

At the dock area in Southampton, we boarded a train without knowing where we would be taken. Eventually, we reached Inverness, the capital of the Scottish Highlands, and then traveled a bit farther to Evanton, which had a closed-down World War II Royal Air Force base.

Again, armed guards escorted us off the train and took us onto the base, which was located on the Cromarty Firth Bay, with runways next to the water. On the other side of the base stood a high mountain, which many of us eventually climbed. From there, you could see the wild, unspoiled beauty of the Highlands; sheep farms and crofters' homes. Nearby, the local Scottish regiment was the queen's own Cameron Highlanders, which had been at the forefront in many wars of protection that England had pursued over hundreds of years.

Once the base in Evanton was opened, the overall purpose of our mission was finally divulged. We set up a lab area and readied our equipment, maintaining very high security. For example, to ensure no radio signals would emanate from the set-up area, we placed all of our electronic equipment inside a room that was entirely enclosed with copper screening. This screened room served as the location where our coded radio systems enabled remote and long-distance radio signals to identify and control the equipment on a 100-foot balloon.

I was responsible for the Electronics Corporation of America electronics package control unit, which controlled the balloon operations and timing. Before launching, I could set the control unit aneroid gauges in a bell jar along with other control unit functions for the flight. The unit had several functions, including controlling the ability to release steel shot from storage boxes on the equipment bar in order to increase the balloon's height. We also controlled the gas that determined the balloon height. All of this was done automatically in flight by the control units after they were programmed and set up while on the ground.

Clearly, wind speeds and direction were critically important in controlling the balloon's path and trajectory and when we would launch. We regularly obtained winds aloft data, which showed that during winter the winds blew from west to east in the Northern Hemisphere. Using calculations, we could estimate how long it would take to get to the Russian border, after which certain high- and low-frequency transmitters could be turned on to remotely track the balloons across the Soviet Union. Simultaneously, we took pictures of the ground with the Chicago aerial camera located in the Boston University package that was attached to the main equipment bar along with the control unit package.

With the basics underway, we were able to investigate our location surroundings. A few miles to the north was a town called Invergordon, also located on the Cromarty Firth but nearer the North Sea than Evanton. At the time, it was a mostly a remote fishing village with a little industry. Today, it is a refurbishment center for North Sea Oil Rig Maintenance, as well as a stopping point for cruise ships, which use its deep-water harbor. Also on the historic Pictish Trail, which runs from Inverness to Golspie and Invergordon, it is known for the beautiful carved stones made by the Pictish people who lived in the area from third to ninth centuries AD. Its Highland history goes back a long way.

While we were there, though, Invergordon was rumored to house a network of communist sympathizers, which only added to our sense of the secrecy and the importance of what we were doing. It's hard to say if those rumors were true, but shortly after we'd arrived, my friend Jim Lloyd was struck and killed by a large truck while walking from the local Evanton train station to our base one night. Whoever caused Jim's death was never found or caught. It might have merely been an accident or the result of a driver who drank one too many pints at the local pub, but it was also at the height of the Cold War. Concern about the expansion of communism was everywhere, and I have always had suspicions that it was not the accident it appeared to be.

To the south of Evanton, before getting to Inverness, was the town of Dingwall. Farther north than Invergordon, at the very tip of Scotland, was Thurso and John O'Groats. These northern towns were near Scappa Flow on the North Sea, opposite the Orkney Islands, where the Germans scuttled their fleet in World War I. Most of these towns had a meeting hall that provided a location for weekly dances for the locals. Once we were launching balloons, our detachment members attended these places frequently. The area rarely got dark in the summer since it was so far north, and farming and fishing were the chief sources of employment, as was a local atomic power station at Dounrey, which is now closed.

Inverness was also the home of Balmoral Castle, one of the Queen of England's summer residences. Some of our detachment made regular trips to Inverness on the weekends, in particular to visit large dance halls/bars called the Meeting Rooms and the Caledonian Hotel. Local girls and those from the remote Highlands loved meeting the Americans, so the dances made the weekend a major attraction for everyone.

In the fall of 1955, we started launching the balloons, with cameras attached, from the base runways next to the Cromarty Firth. Once the hydrogen was in the balloon, the balloon would billow up but be restrained by a heavy clamp over the shroud lines. The shroud lines were connected to the electronics, cameras, and other equipment, which were located on the back of a large truck. When the clamp was removed, the balloon would rise. The truck would drive, following under the balloon before its release. That kept the balloon from dragging equipment on the ground until it reached sufficient altitude, after which we released the clamp. The balloons and equipment would then float upward and east on the prevailing wind and on toward the Soviet Union's borders.

Every launch filled us with excitement and anxiety, since the balloons were filled with explosive hydrogen gas created by hydrogen generators we had installed on the base. One time someone neglected to fasten a ground strap securely to one of the generators that produced the gas, and the static electricity generated between the ground and the ungrounded generator caused a huge explosion that left a 100-foot crater behind.

Based on information from project headquarters located in England, we routinely set the balloons for operations at 80,000 feet. At that height, Russian MIGs and anti-aircraft batteries could not shoot them down and the photographs captured by the Chicago aerial cameras would still show what we wanted. But there were instances when it was necessary to set the controls for 50,000 feet. At that height, the fighter planes could shoot down the balloons. There were even instances when a MIG would detect a low-flying balloon and inadvertently fly into the hydrogen-filled bag, exploding both the plane and the equipment.

We launched hundreds of balloons from five bases in Western Europe, with the expectation that only about 10 percent would get through. After launch, the balloons would drift toward the Far East. Depending on the winds, the trip to the end point would usually take about two to three weeks.

After nearing an estimated pickup point in Southeast Asia, Korea, or Japan, specific radio detectors on our balloon transmitters would identify the secret codes transmitted to local contact points; these were necessary in order to set off dynamite squibs to separate the sub bar from the main bar. The blasts released the camera package, which would then float down on a parachute so a C119 plane could pick up the package while it was still in the air. If the package landed in the water, the plane was equipped with a hook mechanism to retrieve it.

After retrieval, the film packages were sent back to the headquarters base in England for developing and subsequent use by the B-36, B-47, and B-52 bombers in case of war with the Soviet Union. The Russians had moved their industry behind the Ural Mountains during World War II, but our project successfully located their new locations. The equipment employed methods to accurately describe exactly where the photos were taken.

The project name "Grand Union" was used as the code description of the camera and film getting to their designated Far East pickup points. It was a very successful approach, long before Gary Powers' U2 aerial espionage and today's satellite photos were available. We received the Outstanding Unit Citation Award for a Mission Unprecedented in the History of the National Military Establishment for our work. There were many reports in the foreign press of the Soviet Union's complaints about the American balloons and the cameras and electronic equipment contained in them. At one point, the Russians actually brought the equipment to the United Nations to protest the incursions.

At the height of the Cold War, our military needed to know the location of the most important strategic bombing sites in the Soviet Union. The Grand Union project served that purpose. Yet, while the obtained photos were very valuable, the balloons drifted where the winds blew them, which during the winter was from west to the east across the Soviet Union. Eventually, during the spring of 1956, the winds reversed direction and the project was terminated. We packed up the remaining site equipment, dismantled the lab set up, closed the base in Evanton, and returned home to the United States.

Simultaneously, Lockheed's "Skunk Works" in California, under designer Kelly Johnson, was working on the U2, an advanced manned aircraft intended to fly over the Soviet Union (or elsewhere) and take photos of the ground. This new technology was not dependent on wind direction and allowed the military to select their destinations for clandestine photography. In 1957, after Grand Union had been terminated, the United States started flying the manned U2s over the Soviet Union. Because of the planes' very advanced technology, and their altitude and speed capability, the Russians were unable to shoot them down.

The United States flew those missions for several years, until the Russians were finally able to down one of the planes in 1960. It was the famous U2 piloted by Gary Powers. The Russians made a great international furor over the incident and paraded the plane's remnants into the United Nations, along with the pilot. Dwight Eisenhower, then President of the United States, made the original decision to approve these flights, along with then Secretary of State John Foster Dulles and his brother, Allen Dulles, who headed the CIA. Several years later, Powers came home in an exchange for the top Russian spy, Rudolph Able, who had been captured and detained in the United States.

This was the dangerous Cold War environment that John F. Kennedy inherited when he became president in 1960. He also had to confront the Cuban Missile Crisis when the Russians tried to move nuclear missiles into Cuba.

Years later, reconnaissance satellites would take over the role of espionage from the air. In time, the then-fearsome Soviet Union and its communist dictatorship collapsed due to the work of Ronald Reagan and Mikhail Gorbachev, as well as the economic failure of socialism.

Compilation of Domestic and Foreign Press Balloon Reports on Project Grand Union

Cassai, Nello. "Sorry – AF Balloons Carry no Imps, Mice." *Denver Post*, September 14, 1955.

"New Research Balloon Trip Tried." (AP), September 1, 1955.

"Huge Plastic Weather Balloon Launched." *Denver Post*, September 14, 1955.

"Runaway Balloon Stumps Scientists." (UPI), September 1955.

"Lowry Balloon Starts Secret Weapon Talk." *Denver* Post, September 1955 (presumed).

Wulvehill, Tom. "2 Weather Balloons Lofted by USAFE Group." Foreign Press (SS), January 20, 1956.

"Mystery Boxes Fall into France." British News (UPI), February 5, 1956.

"Balloons Launched from Ross-Shire." British News, February 1956.

"U.S. Will Still Launch Balloon." British News, March 1956.

Sohn, John T. "History of 1st Air Division (Study #62)." Headquarters, Strategic Air Command, November 1956.

Johnson, Stanley. "Russia Protests Balloons Flying over Territory." (UPI), February 1956.

"Balloon Vow Given Sweden." (AP), March 13, 1956.

I personally took the following photographs during the balloon espionage project:

Balloon with ballast, electronics, and camera package
attached to parachutes

Balloon on the launch pad

Balloon during launch

Balloon being launched

Balloon with equipment on its way

CHAPTER 3

IBM – The Early Years

After discharge from the air force in March 1957, I remained very interested in electrical engineering. Fortunately, I had the GI Bill to help pay for college. My brother Carl suggested that I apply for a job at IBM, since they could also help pay my tuition. At the time, IBM was advertising opportunities for interviews at their New York City headquarters in the local papers. They were interested in hiring graduate electrical engineers with specialties in electronics.

During the late 1950s, most electrical engineers were of the power school variety, and the number of those with an electronics background was limited. IBM tested graduate engineers to determine their knowledge of electronics and computers, which were still in their infancy and required a specialization quite different from the electrical engineering a utility company would require. Even though I was not a graduate engineer at the time, I passed the test and was sent to the birthplace of IBM—Endicott, New York—to interview. Dan Weiser, the Advanced Technology Department manager, probably hired me for my electronics background and because I had honed up on semiconductor physics before the interview.

I was offered a job with the Time Equipment Division, which wasn't really that interesting to me at the time. Even so, it was a job, and a job with IBM. I started working on relay design and designed a sub program for their automatic production recorder (APR) equipment, which was used to keep track of manufacturing and other operations on the production floor. When an alternate laboratory job opened in the new

Advanced Technology Circuit area, working on semiconductor circuits, I jumped at the opportunity.

During the next five years, I worked directly under two great engineers, Dudley Gill and Ed Pasternak. I was able to participate in the testing and design of early semiconductor logic and memory circuits that would eventually be used for the first time in the new IBM 360 commercial computer systems, then in development using the new Solid Logic Technology (SLT).

Some of the circuits were based on samples that were made at Texas Instruments by Jack Kilby, who later received the Nobel Prize for the integrated circuit. Dudley and I were assigned to develop the electronics for the 1-megabit magnetic drum memory, which was proposed as a replacement for the original memory used in the old IBM 650 computers. As computer usage increased over the years, more memory capacity and speed were increasingly necessary, and that was the purpose of our project.

The original magnetic drum memory used in the IBM 650 machine was becoming too small and too slow for the evolving use of business class computers. Our specific project was to reduce the access time per bit, or, in other words, to speed up the memory, as well as increase the size of the memory. To that end, we designed the electronics and packaging, using semiconductors rather than electron tubes. We also packaged the electronics as close to the magnetic memory drum as possible to cut down on electrical noise and circuit delays.

Dudley was a fine man and a creative engineer, but he decided to go back to school to get his doctorate before the project was completed, so I was asked by the project managers, Len Poch and Bob Schaffer, to finish Dudley's project. Afterward, I was assigned to work for Gene Clapper, who was a polished, self-taught, and prolific inventor. He was also among the first IBM Fellows. Gene became an IBM Fellow in 1963, in the first group to earn the prestigious title—the greatest recognition an engineer or computer scientist at IBM could achieve. I believe he also had the most patents of anyone at IBM at that time.

Gene was an early pioneer in voice recognition and speech synthesis, an early attempt to understand words based on the phoneme associated with the frequencies contained within spoken words. The project was marginally successful, but it turned out that words are also interpreted by people based on preceding and succeeding words—not just by the sound of the words themselves. Back then, we didn't have the memory semiconductor capacity to store the probability of every word's potential usage for interpretation, which is so important and used in today's Dragon and other speech recognition technology. That capability would only come years later.

One time, when Gene was on vacation, I was asked to demonstrate the technology to visiting IBM executives. I was quite worried about the presentation. In front of the executives, I spoke the word "eight" into the electronics, which decoded the word into its phoneme frequency equivalent. After coding the word, I then instructed the electronics to decipher and play back the phoneme version into the original word.

It worked just fine, with the electronics correctly coded, and decoded the word "eight." After the excited executives left, I went through the same process using the word "six." The electronics responded by saying the word "eight." When Gene returned from vacation, he was relieved to hear the results of the presentation, and the project was identified as a new business-class opportunity for IBM. We could only count ourselves lucky that the executives didn't ask for another example.

These years were a time of considerable growth and opportunity for me. I was fortunate to be able to continue my engineering education both in the classroom and on the job. I was also asked by John Clark, the administrative assistant to the head of the laboratory's Advanced Technology area, to substitute for him in his job during his vacation. That required gathering and forecasting the multimillion-dollar lab technology budgets for the area. It was a new challenge for me and opened up some areas of assignment that I had not previously considered.

Once again, it seemed I was in the right place at the right time. And it certainly was the right time to be entering the computer industry. I benefitted substantially from my interaction with the most highly placed executives, both at the division and corporate levels. I was also entrusted with the responsibility of keeping track of a huge multimillion-dollar budget for the first time in my career.

During the early 1960s, IBM decided to invest huge sums of money into the new technologies planned for the "Bet Your Company" 360 Systems Technology for commercial computer products. The name of the project reflected IBM's mammoth financial gamble, requiring the worldwide integration of new semiconductor technology as well as the attendant electronic packaging and manufacturing. IBM invested enormous amounts of money in manufacturing and development to implement technologies that we planned for use at every scale, from small business-class computers to the very largest computer installations.

This project was also an effort to design commercial computer products that would run software transparently on any of those systems, regardless of size or complexity. In short, IBM was initiating a worldwide endeavor to revolutionize product development, sales, marketing, and manufacturing with engineering prototypes designed in the United States, United Kingdom, and Germany.

By this time, Les Adams had been appointed the electronic packaging czar at IBM headquarters in Endicott by senior technology corporate executive Erich Bloch. I was honored when Les asked me to become his staff assistant to help in the development of this new and emerging technology.

The corporate Solid Logic Technology responsibility for the entire corporate program was located in East Fishkill, New York, under Erich's leadership. There, the new semiconductors were being invented and manufactured. He also appointed two others to work with Les: Dr. Ed Davis for Logic Semiconductors in East Fishkill and Dr. Paul Low for semiconductor memory in Burlington, Vermont.

This great opportunity was also a terrific challenge. In my opinion, it was IBM's "moon shot." We were at the ground floor of both the development of advanced electronic packaging design and the manufacturing of that technology. The high-volume manufacturing of these electronic packaging products was initially under Ed Garvey, who led the IBM Manufacturing Research Lab in Endicott, New York. It was such a hotbed of integration between systems technology design and the technology itself, as well as its manufacturing, that the personal pressures on all of us were enormous.

During the early and mid-1960s, IBM was competing aggressively, in particular with the CDC 6600, a successful machine by Control Data Corporation (CDC) that used their version of an advanced packaging technology. In response, IBM assembled worldwide teams of people to develop new systems ranging in size from the small 360/30 cost performance machine for small applications, being developed in Endicott, New York, to much larger, higher-performance systems being developed at IBM Poughkeepsie, IBM Hursley in England, and IBM Boeblingen in Germany.

Anticipating a huge volume of demand in the business world, cost-performance machines were developed because cost was the most important driver in closing sales. This was a new business opportunity that complemented that smaller but important sector of the market where utilizing very large computers was the highest priority. Teams from all these areas converged on IBM Endicott and the other SLT locations during these years. It was truly a company-wide effort with tens of thousands of people involved across the world.

IBM executives clearly realized that in order to remain competitive on a worldwide basis, a long-range global strategy had to be developed—one that integrated new and emerging technologies with system designs that spanned from small systems to larger, more powerful systems all able to run the same software. In order to do this, new technologies had to be manufactured worldwide and those technologies had to be unique to IBM and developed in-house. IBM could not use the same purchased technology that its competitors used and still remain competitive in terms of the essential cost and performance leverage. Thus, IBM initiated the Solid Logic Technology program and its follow-up versions to achieve this.

SLT was quite a change from the older vacuum tube and the following standard modular system (SMS) technologies, which used discrete semiconductors attached to one-layer paper epoxy printed circuit cards in use in IBM machines prior to 1965. It was exciting, but highly competitive and demanding as well. When the packaging program began to fall behind schedule, Les Adams was transferred to California to work on other products and Ray Rinne was appointed to take his place as the head of the electronic packaging area. I became Ray's staff assistant and began a long and valuable association that has lasted for many years.

Simply stated, electronic packaging is the physical environment that houses the semiconductor chips, chip carriers and printed circuits, cabling, and cooling of these electronic devices in its operating computer environment. Important technical considerations included the conductivity of the metallizations at all levels, how physically close and electrically noisy they were at very high frequencies, and how hot they ran. (The conductivity is the step in the manufacturing process where circuits are interconnected with metals or alloys.), Thus, the closeness of the semiconductors to each other as well as to the electronic packaging environment is essential to the speed of the technology.

The density and volume of the different patterns of all these connections in turn required the development of automatic design automation wiring tools for the interconnection patterns between the assemblies. Our much smaller and denser packaging connections required the development of new and complex ceramic modules, printed circuits and attendant cables, connectors, movable mechanical gates to house all the hardware, and also the cooling of the assemblies in a normal business office environment.

The semiconductor devices IBM used were developed internally in East Fishkill and Burlington, along with the single- and multi-chip ceramic substrates that supported these new semiconductor devices. Initially, these small pressed-ceramic substrates, or single-chip carriers, were built at IBM East Fishkill. The evolutionary strategy of this technology was designed to carry the company far into the future. More importantly, it could not be duplicated outside IBM, much like the old Carrol presses used to originally manufacture the IBM punched cards. These high-volume presses were so unique that eventually, by consent decree, the U.S. Government required that IBM sell the machines to competitors since the Carrol press technology was so difficult and complicated to manufacture.

Over more than two decades, IBM had evolved proprietary technologies for mainframe computers that were unique to the company and could not be manufactured elsewhere. These included Solid Logic Technology and, ultimately, thermal conduction multilayer multi-chip ceramic technology, which included the printed circuit board packaging, Freon cooling, and all the testing and manufacturing required. It was a worldwide and hugely successful enterprise costing enormous sums of money.

This technology provided the cost and performance leverage that IBM needed to successfully lead the industry at the time. As history shows, the IBM competitors that existed in the hugely profitable mainframe computer business in the 1950s, 1960s, and 1970s have largely disappeared. The Japanese computer manufacturers (JCM) with IBM software that would run on the JCM machines were among the few mainframe survivors.

CHAPTER 4

Tom Watson Jr., and the Dawn of my Competitive Analysis and the CDC 6600

One day in 1965, my manager, Ray Rinne, came to my office at IBM Endicott and asked me to meet someone. He introduced me to Tom Watson Jr., the president and chairman of IBM who was visiting Endicott to view the electronic packaging area planned for the new SLT and 360 System product line.

Mr. Watson was a tall, distinguished gentleman and the son of Tom Watson Sr., the original president of IBM from the 1920s to the 1950s. During the early 1960s, one of IBM's principal competitors was CDC. Mr. Watson asked me if I knew anything about the CDC 6600 machine technology. I said that I didn't but offered to gather all the information I could. Ray and Mr. Watson told me to make that a priority.

This was my introduction to competitive analysis, also known as corporate espionage. That meant the first thing I had to do was to get my hands on a CDC 6600 to examine and analyze it. Truth is, I was intrigued by the assignment. It was my first in my new position as an associate engineer and a real chance to concentrate on a competitive analysis study.

But in order to respond to Mr. Watson's request, I had to come up with a way to see and examine the CDC 6600 technology. Jack Rogers, senior executive of IBM Data Processing at Armonk Corporate Headquarters, provided me with a list of facilities where both CDC 6600s and IBM machines were installed. My next step was to devise a strategy for getting in the door to see the rival equipment.

Jack's office originally provided me with four joint-customer names, along with the branch office and name of the IBM salesman for each account. The four accounts were located in New York City (Computech and New York University), Washington, D.C. (the Weather Bureau), and Los Angeles (Aerospace). Later, we also learned of joint accounts at Lawrence Livermore Labs in California and the University of California, Berkeley campus. I decided to try to visit the Livermore Labs facility first.

Our first venture into corporate espionage was almost too easy. Ray Rinne and I gained entry to the labs in the evening, when only one CDC technician employee was on-site. While our visit was ostensibly to look at the IBM equipment, I eventually got around to asking the CDC employee about the nearby CDC 6600 equipment. He never suspected the real purpose of our visit and was quite helpful. He even opened the covers on the CDC 6600 equipment so we were able to get a closer look at the pluggable CDC field replaceable unit (FRU), which contained the circuits and components.

We removed some of the computer cards and took photographs of all that we could get access to, including the components, connectors, cabling, and cooling. The obliging CDC employee volunteered even more information about the number of discrete wires and engineering changes associated with the equipment and components, the circuit speed, and the machine performance. I couldn't blame him for his enthusiasm. Our shared field was still so new and so specialized that it was hard to find another "geek" who understood the intricacies of the technology; he must have seen us as kindred spirits.

We returned home and prepared opinion reports on CDC's technology and how it compared to the IBM SLT technology, finally presenting the results to Mr. Watson, who was very pleased with our information.

Our opinion at the time was that the CDC technology, while adequate for the 6600 and possibly some later versions, was probably not as cost competitive as IBM's SLT technology; it used older, discrete components and required more labor for assembly. It also wouldn't be able to deliver the number of machines that IBM had anticipated it would sell, and IBM's standardized SLT technology could be integrated and manufactured within IBM worldwide.

The initial IBM 360 machines used three copper balls attached to the semiconductors for connection to the ceramic substrates since there was only one circuit per semiconductor chip at that time. By comparison, today's chips contain many, many more circuits per chip. Back in the 1960s, IBM had evolving and emerging technologies that included advanced semiconductors, complex printed circuits, and ceramic multilayer multi-chip module substrates, plus a proprietary semiconductor interconnection process called controlled collapse chip connection (C4), which was unique to IBM and patented.

These multi-chip and multilayer ceramics represented a new and unique way of connecting semiconductors to the underlying connection substrate, and a giant step toward using the advanced chips we have today. It was the origin of the far-reaching benefits for generations of new IBM products and technology that CDC did not have. This C4 process enabled semiconductor chips to have multiple I/O solder pads on them and could be used to automatically connect many circuits per chip to the next level. IBM technology was also manufactured in-house and therefore not as dependent on purchased technology and components, as CDC's was.

By the end of the CDC report, I was convinced that the kind of competitive analysis work I had done was just the tip of the iceberg. For better or worse, I knew corporate espionage was essential to IBM's staying ahead of its competitors. Further, my ability to do this work put me in contact with the highest levels of management, and that could only be to my long-term benefit. Add to that the virtual disappearance of U.S. companies like Sperry Rand, Univac, RCA, Burroughs, Control Data, Digital Equipment, Data General, and others, and I had all the evidence I needed to know that this work was critical to our survival.

Years later, CDC would sue IBM for unfair competition. We heard that CDC reportedly spent huge sums and much time gathering IBM documents through a massive data collection effort to build their claim. In many ways, it was like my experiences during the Cold War, only what were then huge governments were now huge companies, locked in a struggle for power.

Some of my competitive study documents were even part of CDC's very strong case. Eventually, IBM settled with CDC when Ronald Reagan became president and a new attorney general was put in place. Part of the settlement was that CDC turn over all of the documents it had gathered, legally or illegally, to IBM. Once IBM received those documents, they were entirely and immediately destroyed.

Interestingly enough, at the same time, IBM was also being sued by the Federal Government on antitrust charges. From what I heard, when the U.S. Government found out that all of the CDC documents were destroyed after Reagan became president, they dropped their case against IBM, as reported in the *New York Times* on January 9, 1982.

DON FRANCK

Richard E. Imershein
Old Orchard Road, Armonk, New York 10504

March 12, 1970

Dear Don,

Thank you very much for your very interesting presentation. I am sure that as a result you have opened additional lines of communication.

Again, our thanks.

Sincerely,

R. E. Imershein

cc: Mr. R. A. Rinne

Mr. D. R. Franck
IBM Corporation
Endicott, New York

RICHARD IMERSHEIN WAS HEAD OF
IBM WORLD WIDE COMPETITIVE ANALYSIS

DEEP BLUE

SPD HQ – White Plains
44 South Broadway
27/630   16S-21
August 5, 1980

MEMORANDUM TO: Mr. D. Franck

Don, thank you very much for the Split Rock workshop report. I found it very interesting.

J. D. Kuehler

JDK/ahr

JACK KUEHLER, PRESIDENT OF IBM, WAS REFERRING TO MY IEEE
REPORT CONCERNING COMPETITVE TECHNOLOGY

DON FRANCK

C. B. Rogers, Jr.
875 Johnson Ferry Road, N.E., Atlanta, Georgia 30342

January 26, 1973

Dear Don,

I am looking forward to hearing your presentation on the status of the Japanese computer industry and appreciate your participation on such short notice in our staff meeting January 30, 1973. Your reservations are confirmed at the Executive Park Hotel for guaranteed late arrival Monday, January 29.

Sincerely,

Mr. D. R. Franck
IBM Corporation
Department P73, Building 40/2
P. O. Box 6
Endicott. New York 13760

Jack Rogers was President of IBM Sales and Service

SPD HEADQUARTERS
38-636/2G 55
Extension 6-7634
July 29, 1974

MEMORANDUM TO: Mr. D. R. Franck

SUBJECT: Competitive Technology Report
                   1973-1978

Don, thank you for sending me a copy of the subject report.
It's a nice piece of work and one of the few documents that
I actually enjoy browsing through.

E. M. Davis

EMD:bd

DR.ED DAVIS WAS ONE OF THE PRESIDENTS OF CIRCUIT AND
SEMICONDUCTOR DEVELOPPMENT AT IBM EAST FISHKILL NY.

DON FRANCK

CD - HARRISON
Dept. 33-630 Loc: 2G
Telephone: 8-254-4608
October 25, 1971

MEMORANDUM TO: Mr. D. R. Franck
                    Mr. J. S. Jephson

SUBJECT: Packaging Competitive Analysis

Your inputs last week were of great help to us in understanding our
present strengths and weaknesses and in projecting them forward to
the FS time frame. We were very impressed with the detail
and completeness of your work. We need similarly integrated and
well thought out analysis in other areas of our technology.

Thanks very much for your help.

                              G. R. Gunther-Mohr

GRGM/mlg

cc: Dr. R. E. Gomory
    Mr. L. O. Hill
    Mr. R. A. Rinne

G.R. GUNTHER-MOHR WAS THE SENIOR TECHNOLOGY REPRESENTATIVE
FOR DR.GOMORY WHO WAS PRESIDENT OF IBM's RESEARCH DIVISION

31

P. A. Toole
IBM Corporation, Endicott, N. Y.

January 26, 1979

Dear Don,

The CMC meeting on panels was extremely successful.
The information which you helped compile was received with
great interest by the CMC.

I would like to personally thank you for your efforts in
this regard.

Sincerely,

P. A. Toole

THE CMC WAS THE IBM CORPORATE MANAGEMENT COMMITTEE.
IT WAS TYPICALLY COMPOSED OF THE TOP 4 CORPORATE IBM EXECUT
INCLUDING THE PRESIDENT OF IBM

General Technology Division

Presents to

Donald R. Franck

A Division Award

in appreciation and recognition for

Worldwide Vendor Survey

July 25, 1985

Edward m Davis

Division President

Patrick A. Toole

Site General Manager

DEEP BLUE

SPERRY ⊕ UNIVAC

P.O. BOX 500
BLUE BELL, PENNSYLVANIA 19424
TELEPHONE (215) 542-4011

June 5, 1980

Mr. Don Franck
IBM Department V55
1701 North Street
Endicott, NY 13760

Dear Don:

On behalf of the IEEE Computer Society Technical
Committee on Packaging, I would like to thank you
for serving as a session chairman at our bi-annual
workshop held on May 28th through May 30th, 1980.

The session you arranged on System Design Impact
on Technology certainly was of high caliber and
very pertinent to the entire workshop theme. All
your speakers did an outstanding job, and you
maintained good control and ran a very timely
session.

Again thank you - your efforts made this workshop a
resounding success.

                    Sincerely,

                    D..I. Amey

DIA/mal

DON FRANCK

IEEE COMPUTER SOCIETY

OFFICE OF THE PRESIDEI
Tse-yun Fei
Department of Computer Scien
Wright State Universi
Dayton, Ohio 454:
Telephone: (513) 873-24!

January 2, 1980

Mr. Donald R. Franzk
DV 13/B 0402
IBM Corporation
Endicott, NY 13760

Dear Mr. Franzk:

I am delighted to confirm your appointment as Chairman of the
Computer Packaging (TC). As this appointment carries the responsibility
for the technical vitality of the IEEE Computer Society in this area -
as well as a significant personal commitment - we will try to support
you in whatever ways we can in developing and conducting your technical
program.

Organizationally you are responsible to the Vice President of the
Systems Technology Technical Interest Council (TIC), Oscar Garcia.
As a TC Chairman you are an ex-officio member of the Society's
Governing Board and a member of Systems Technology TIC. As in the past,
the Technical Interest Councils will meet three times a year at major
computer conference sites. We hope that you will be able to attend
as many of these meetings as possible, but we expect some representation
from your committee at each of our meetings. Oscar will coordinate
the appropriate technical reporting and the Society's support with you.

We are pleased to welcome you to our Technical Committee leadership
and look forward to our Computer Society association.

Sincerely,

Tse-yun Feng

cc: Oscar Garcia
     Harry Hayman

TF/kag

35

IEEE COMPUTER SOCIETY

OFFICE OF THE PRESIDENT

Dr. Richard E. Merwin
IEEE Computer Society
1109 Spring Street, Suite 201
Silver Spring, Maryland 20910
(202) 676-4951
(301) 589-3386

February 10, 1981

Mr. Don Franck
IBM Corporation
Dept. V55/0402
1701 North Street
Endicott, NY 13760

Dear Don:

It is my pleasure to reappoint you for the term ending December 31, 1981, to serve as chairman of the IEEE Computer Society Technical Committee on Computer Packaging.

As you know, the technical committees form the technical backbone of the Computer Society. Your leadership and participation in this assignment is crucial to the continued service to our membership and Society growth.

Your service in the past as TC chairman is deeply appreciated and Ed Parrish and I look forward to working with you in 1981.

Sincerely,

Richard Merwin

Richard E. Merwin
President
IEEE Computer Society

REM/gpk

cc: E. Parrish

INSTITUTE OF ELECTRICAL AND ELECTRONICS ENGINEERS

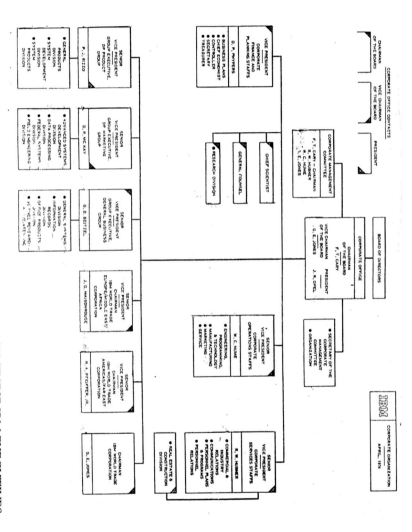

D. FRANCK PRESENTED HIS COMPETITION ANALYSIS TO THESE IBM EXECUTIVES.

CHAPTER 5

Competitive Technology Evaluation Methods

As we continued our exploits investigating our competitors, both the pace and the need for greater and greater amounts of information intensified. We couldn't continue to depend, as we had at CDC, on a loose-lipped employee or simple luck. I had to develop a whole methodology for finding out what we needed to know.

As always, the IBM senior executives had the same essential questions:

What is the technology used in competing products?

How does the competitors' technology compare to IBM's?

What are the costs and performances of the competitors' products?

Who are the manufacturers of the competitors' technology?

What are the competitors' strengths and weaknesses versus IBM's?

What are the supplier industry costs for such technology?

What resources did the competitors have to compete with IBM?

Initially at least I found that I could answer all these questions by becoming familiar with the competition via trade show displays, technical meetings, computer conferences, published reports, and other public and professional means. Later, the questions were geared more toward what would or might happen in the future. That was always a much more difficult scenario to envision, but it was very important since it had to do with the timing and investments that IBM had to make today in order to remain competitive at the box level in the future.

Answering questions about the competitive environment required my gathering information from many different areas. For the semiconductors, I sought out information from companies like Texas Instruments, Fairchild, Motorola, Intel, and others emerging in the market. For connectors, I went primarily to AMP, Berg, and Cinch Graphic. For cabling, it was the Rogers Corporation and others. These manufacturers and the IBM system product competitors had changed a great deal over the years, with some new companies and competitors coming to the fore, such as the JCMs and Amdahl Corporation.

That period also saw the virtual disappearance of many heretofore well-known and respected computer competitors like RCA, Burroughs, and Honeywell. These companies had good technologies but not the broad and worldwide product and technology design, manufacturing capability, and financial strength that IBM developed. Computer technology was increasingly becoming a global market, and to dominate that market meant a company almost had to have global reach.

For me, personal and professional networking became a particularly effective tool in conducting underground corporate research. Sometimes it really is not just *what* you know, but *who* you know. My best sources for data came from trade shows and professional society meetings, publications, and independent consultants. All these sources were particularly helpful. I am a lifetime member of the Institute of Electrical Engineers (IEEE) and have been a member for more than fifty years. As the largest organization of its kind in the world, my IEEE association gave me access to many technical professionals employed by IBM competitors.

As a member of the IEEE, I was able to participate in professional society meetings and use my association and eventual role as chairman of the Technical Committee on Computer Packaging to understand and gather world-class technical information. There were many competing companies whose representatives participated in our meetings, but our technical discussions were invariably about the technical merits, advantages, shortcomings, and disadvantages of various technologies and technical approaches.

As chairman, I was able to make contacts, and set up and encourage members across the globe to participate in our meetings and submit technical papers for potential presentation. These were available to all participating members.

These days, most people outside the industry tend to take their computer technology for granted. They have only a vague idea of how computers work and tend to get frustrated when they don't. But in the days when the forerunners of today's machines were under development, we walked the razor's edge of mutual professional respect for our colleagues and truly cutthroat competition. New developments, however small, could constitute a breakthrough of major proportions. So there was almost a manic interest in the technical information and status of U.S., Japanese, and European technologies, especially in the mainframe computer technology business.

Because a major portion of IBM's revenue came from mainframe sales, that's what the technology corporate executives were most focused on at the time. However, in the early 1980s, IBM's development and announcement of their personal computer (PC) ignited a new chapter in IBM's history and in the world, that eventually became a barn burner in sales for many smaller companies. Paul Carroll's book *Big Blues: The Unmaking of IBM* presents an accurate picture of how IBM fumbled a huge new opportunity to dominate this business after its initial and unique announcement of the IBM PC.

International Business Machines Corporation

Office of the Vice President
System Products Division

1000 Westchester Avenue, White Plains, N.Y. 10604

September 18, 1974

Dear Don,

Congratulations! You are one of a group of selected SPD
technical professionals, some in management positions, who
have been invited to the SPD Engineering Symposium at the
Cerromar Beach Hotel, Puerto Rico, November 18-21, 1974.

You have been picked by your management in recognition of
the quality and consistency of your work and because of
demonstrated ability to contribute in a major way to SPD's
development efforts.

The Symposium is a forum devoted to the exchange of timely
information about the business and our engineering programs.
We plan to provide a series of presentations on the job
facing us over the next few years, and a chance to take part
in several interactive technical exchanges. There also will
be time for recreation.

Attached is a general information sheet and a recreation
questionnaire. Please fill out the questionnaire and return
it to the address shown as soon as possible.

I look forward to seeing you in Puerto Rico.

Sincerely,

D. J. Gavis

Mr. D. R. Franck
D/U13, Bldg. 040-2
Endicott

the pathfinders

DON FRANCK
name

System Products Division
Engineering Symposium
Cerromar Beach Hotel
Puerto Rico
November 18-21, 1974

SPD

During the years I was active at IEEE, I made many friends, regularly attended and participated in many technical meetings, and, as a senior engineer representing IBM, contributed to the professionalism of our IEEE technical committee. I was also elected to the board of the International Electronic Packaging Society, which allowed me to forge many personal relationships with our competitors' engineers. When I was assigned to the Agenda Planning Committee, I was able to evaluate many competitive technical papers before publication and to lead discussions about competitors' and IBM technology.

While none of this might be considered corporate espionage, per se, it did place huge amounts of relatively exclusive information at my disposal. In addition, I was able to arrange visits to key laboratories in Japan, such as Kyocera, the Ministry of International Trade and Industry (MITI), Nippon Telephone & Telegraph (NTT), Nippon Electronics Company (NEC), Hitachi, and Fujitsu.

On one occasion while in Japan, I had a personal dinner with Dr. Leo Esaki, who shared the Nobel Prize for physics for electron tunneling and who also invented the Esaki diode. Later, in 1967, Leo became an IBM Fellow at the Watson Research Lab, where his first paper (covering the semiconductor super lattice) was published by IBM.

Meetings at trade shows and professional meetings sometimes necessitated the occasional clandestine taping of conversations and presentations. Other times, I sometimes photographed significant technology on display. Along with some other colleagues and regular attendees at worldwide trade shows, we formed a group called the Basic Family Unit (BFU), where we would exchange information that was not company confidential or proprietary, for our mutual professional benefit. IBM was not aware of some of these activities at the time. In my own mind, I was doing what was necessary to participate with fellow professionals in an ethical and forthright manner.

Yet because of so much interest from senior IBM executives and others in competitive analysis, and specific companies and products, we had to establish a competitive analysis (CA) technology room in Endicott. It was there that we housed competitive hardware, descriptions and photographs of important and interesting products, and other information.

The precedent had been set years earlier by Hap Fisher at IBM San Jose, in what is now known as Silicon Valley. There, he was responsible for disc storage products. He bought and ran competitive equipment and did extensive studies of costs, reliability, and performance of competitors' equipment in his CA lab. John Keffer collected similar data for printer products in his Endicott lab operations. As such, I was able to assist and collaborate many times within these areas of technology evaluation.

At Endicott, we had every kind of competitor product under our microscope. The various displays contained in the CA technology room (that I had set up and for which I was responsible) incorporated a full range of products both available and in development at the time and manufactured around the globe.

Some examples follow:

Digital Equipment Cards	Melcom 70 Card	Burroughs B80 Card
Honeywell 60/36 Mini	Hazeltine Display	CDC Omega 480
Acos Nec Technology –samples	Fujitsu Follow-On	Amdahl 470 V6
Cray-1 – samples & photos	CDC 203	Hitachi Disc Controller
HP 3000 CPU Mini	HP 2631 Printer	Honeywell 66/85
ICL Array Processor	Hitachi Technology (1968–1985)	

In addition, I had samples in a commodity section, displaying supplier connector products from Berg Electronics and Cinch Graphic, as well as printed circuits from various manufacturers. Other products on display were Pactel polyimide substrate, Jedec substrates, Multiwire, Shoebox Zif packaging, cabling, and others items of current interest. I had a complete display of Amp connectors as well. All of these products could be easily analyzed for pricing, and manufacturers were always eager to sell their products to IBM. At the same time, many of these products were used in competitive equipment and sold to other manufacturers. To build my cost estimates then, it was just a matter of knowing which parts were used in which competitor machines.

Our database collections also helped with the forecasting of future technologies, which I'll go into in more detail in later chapters. To establish a basis of future forecasts for technology parameters, I traced the first customer ship dates as a means of identifying when a particular technology was first used in a competing product. That established a firm time basis for the component.

The technology had to actually be used in a competing product and not just seen in a laboratory or talked about at a trade show or professional society meeting. The genius of the method was that the data could only be used once and not counted again if used in subsequent products. My consequent plotting of actual data and the statistical results of the actual plotted data could then be applied to the forecasts for five to twenty years in the future, and showed statistical correlation factors in the 90 percent or above range. I only used data I gathered myself, so any scatter due to errors was minimized.

CHAPTER 6

The Amdahl Corporation 470/V6

Gene Amdahl was an IBM employee and eventually became a prestigious IBM Fellow. Initially, he worked on the IBM 704 and 709 computers, which used, respectively, vacuum tubes and the IBM SMS discrete component hardware. But despite his accomplishments, Gene was never entirely a "company man." He left IBM in December 1955, but returned again in 1960 to work on the System/360 family architecture.

In 1965 he became an IBM fellow and was made head of the IBM Advanced Computer Systems (ACS) lab in Menlo Park, California. Gene left IBM again in 1970 to start his own Amdahl Computer Company with eventual financial help from Fujitsu. He designed a very fast computer called the 470-V6 using advanced packaging and semiconductors. He also reportedly coined the term "fud," which was an acronym for "the fear, uncertainty, and doubt" that IBM sales people would instill in the minds of potential customers who might be considering Amdahl products.

Gene created a unique, high-performance uniprocessor that was "plug compatible" with IBM software products used in the 370/168. In short, it would run IBM customer programs, so it gave customers an alternative to buying IBM, since their 360/370 application software would work on the Amdahl machine for less money. In addition, there were other instructions in the Amdahl machine that, if used or added to the customers' programs, insured that the software would not work back on the IBM machines.

By 1975, a great deal of corporate worry about the Amdahl 470-V6 existed, so I was asked to put together a technology comparison for

IBM executive management. I gathered published reports and used my contacts in the professional society meetings to gain a good knowledge of the technology used in the 470-V6. It was impressive. But we were still not sure of the computer's uniprocessor cycle times and circuit speed, so I surreptitiously visited Gene's company in California to see what additional information I could gather. Corporate espionage can get creative, and mine certainly did.

Fortunately, or unfortunately, I discovered that Amdahl had disposed of a number of technology-filled boxes that were placed on public land to be picked up by local garbage companies. This was long before our current regulations that require computer equipment to be disposed of or recycled in very specific ways. When I found those files, I could barely contain my excitement. They turned out to contain the very circuit delay data I needed, which I sent on to interested parties in East Fishkill and elsewhere in IBM. During this time, IBM also wanted to run benchmark software on the Amdahl 470-V6, and I was again asked to evaluate the technology that was used in Amdahl equipment.

IBM Data Processing Headquarters found a joint account in Melbourne, Australia, that also had IBM systems installed. So a team was assembled to do an on-site evaluation in Australia. I had returned from California and was in Japan at the time, so I flew from Japan to the Philippines, then on to Australia to meet the rest of the team. I arrived on a Friday, but no team was in sight. By Monday, I was getting worried about the project since no one had contacted me about how to proceed.

That same Monday, I was able to get in touch with the IBM branch office manager. Surprisingly, he said the project had been delayed for several months. So, making the best of a bad situation, I decided to stay on for a tour of Australia before returning home. It may not have benefitted IBM, but proved a most interesting trip for me personally.

By 1979, Amdahl had sold over $1 billion of V6 and V7 mainframes and had 6,000 employees worldwide. They went on to develop the IBM plug-compatible front end processor (the 4705) as well as high-performance disk drives, both jointly created with Fujitsu engineers.

For those readers with an interest in technical detail, I share as an example the original logic circuit and packaging technology used in the 470-V6 below. All of the data for the competitive hardware that I gathered over the years for any company in the computer business competing against IBM always included the first customer ship date for that hardware in a machine that had actually shipped to a customer.

As I said previously, that date is key since it enabled the standardized time-based forecasting of competitors' technology used in shipped machines, as discussed in later chapters. This provided a quantitative technology forecasting tool that was quite useful and essential. It could then be used to set our own internal First Customer Ship (FCS) system schedule targets in order to remain competitive. Those FCS targets could also be used to set internal technology schedule dates for manufacturing and development.

Company:	Amdahl
Product:	470-V6
First Customer Ship date:	05/1975
MIPS (millions of instruction/second)	2.5 estimated
Processor Cycle Time:	65 nanoseconds
Circuits per chip:	65
I/Os per chip:	84
Circuit Performance:	0.75 NS
Chip Size: in mm^2	4.5
Circuit Power in MW:	35
Chips per Module:	1
Module Size:	0.5 x 0.5"
Circuits/FRU (Field Replaceable Unit):	2500
FRU I/O Grid (inches/qty):	0.05 in w/800
FRU Conductor Width (inches):	5 mils on 0.062 Grid
FRU Size (inches):	7.5 x 7.5

CHAPTER 7

Gaining the Advantage – The Worldwide Printed Circuit Vendor Survey

For several years, there was an ongoing controversy about the competitiveness of the IBM Endicott plant's Printed Circuit Board (PCB) manufacturing costs. Even so, there was never any doubt about its ability to manufacture in huge volumes with very advanced PCB technology that other vendors couldn't match. From the mid-1960s through the early 1980s, most of my studies showed a gradual increase in the ability of the independent printed circuit manufacturers, who supplied products to end users, to increase their technical capability.

These independent PCB suppliers were always cheaper than IBM for simple printed circuits like paper epoxy and two-layer epoxy glass printed circuits with one line per channel on a 0.100 grid. In addition, the merchant supplier industry tooled up their manufacturing lines for much larger panel sizes than IBM's.

In situations where PCBs are relatively small and difficult to process individually, manufacturers produce many of them in large panels. When a number of identical circuits are printed onto a larger panel, they can then be handled normally. The panel is broken apart into individual PCBs when all other processing is complete. Separating the individual PCBs is frequently aided by drilling or routing perforations along the boundaries of the individual circuits, much like a sheet of postage stamps.

Typically, the industry panel size was around 15 x 15 inches, while IBM's was 10 x 15 inches, as originally established for the IBM SLT program in 1965. That had been a huge investment by IBM in order to handle the standardized volumes of printed circuits required with multiple layers and two to three lines per channel.

Some of IBM's competitors in the computer business, like Data General, were buying larger panels from their merchant PCB industry suppliers in that time period, but these had less complexity in layers and lines per channel than those produced by IBM. So, in order to be competitive with IBM at the common circuit speeds, they used fewer parts and connectors. This choice turned out to be limiting in the long term, as demands for faster circuits grew, along with increased density and wire ability on the PCBs. For more complex products and mainframe applications, the complexity of IBM PCBs enabled superior performance. That was where IBM was very strong and competitive—rather than in cost efficiency, which was the strength of those manufacturers of simple PCBs.

Still, the 10 x 15-inch panel size limitation at IBM Endicott became an issue in the mid-1970s, especially for the high-volume backup tooling then being set up at IBM Austin (Texas), which was supposed to duplicate that of IBM Endicott. As older programs began to approach eventual obsolescence, Endicott tooled up for sizes as large as 24 x 28 inches with very fine conductors and twenty-four layers. This PCB was used to attach and interconnect the 100-chip thermal conduction multi-chip (TCM) modules with the same Freon cooling used in the high-performance mainframes like the IBM 3081 with a first customer computer product ship in December 1981.

No one in the industry then or even today could make those complex printed circuits in volume. As a result of some ongoing internal competitive debates about costs and technical complexity, a worldwide executive review was commissioned to tour the PCB manufacturers in the Far East, Southeast Asia, the United States, and Europe. I was a member of the three-person team that made that trip and report. We were all awarded a General Technology Division President's Award on July 25, 1983, for the study and our results, which helped determine our competitive position, cost, and technical capability status.

In summary, IBM was able to manufacture in huge quantities far more complex printed circuits than the competition, enabling the interconnection of many more circuits, ICs (integrated circuits), and modules on its printed circuit boards. That in turn enabled IBM to use fewer, more highly reliable parts to implement a computer box at a lower cost than anyone else in the business.

IBM had gained a major competitive technical advantage for these complicated boards, but was largely non-competitive when simple PCBs were required. Since a huge volume of IBM revenue was derived from the sale of large high-performance computers, that technology was usually too expensive for small electronic products or computers that used a lesser technology, so IBM was not as competitive in that area. But things were about to change.

CHAPTER 8

The Japanese Competitive Analysis Technology Training Program

By 1973, it was apparent to me and the executives at IBM that a more pervasive worldwide competitive analysis organization had to be established if we were to gather the necessary competitive data, make comparisons, and accurately forecast. That was the only way to remain competitive.

Why was that so important? Because when doing business on a global scale, a world of information is needed, and that need for information had grown beyond the ability of just a few of us to supply it. The future of computer technology was coming hard upon us, and we needed to stay ahead in order to survive.

Our prime needs, in descending order of importance, were these:

1. We needed to provide professional predictions of at least three to five years, showing the directions for internal IBM product design and the corresponding technology in quantified technical terms. This was necessary in order to provide resources, establish internal measurements, and take proper technical steps to optimize product development. Investments in technology had to be made early enough (sometimes many years in advance) to allow the new technology to be manufactured, tested, and shipped to the end-customer at the required first customer ship date to meet or beat the competition.

2. We needed to compare "shipped" technology. Sometimes our information was obtained too late to impact internal IBM product designs. But over time, the data would become part of a compounded data bank able to help us predict trends to accomplish the first priority above.

3. We lacked necessary new business studies that would permit the possible introduction of new technologies and products to expand our product base to offset decreasing order volumes that had resulted from advances such as large-scale integration and other business trends.

4. Large scale integration represented a giant step in manufacturing. Earlier, a component like a semiconductor chip might have one circuit per chip, which we would employ in small circuit integration. In an application, it might require 10,000 circuits to implement a final product. That meant we would need 10,000 chips, along with the attendant chip carriers, printed circuits, cabling, and other technology, to create a finished box product to be shipped to a customer.

On the other hand, when we could manufacture a chip with 5,000 circuits on it, then we'd only need two chips to implement the functionality required. While the 5,000-circuit chip would surely be more expensive than a one-circuit chip, it would still be more cost effective to implement than the one-circuit solution, which would require substantially more chips in the final box product utilizing this kind of large-scale integration. In this case, it would also require far fewer chip carriers and printed circuits to implement than the one-circuit solution. We had to be aware of the effect of such advances and the demand for them well before they arrived on the market. Our data-bank intelligence made that possible, but we needed to increase our knowledge base.

At the time, many competitive factors were affecting IBM growth and income, both in current and future time frames, including sales situations, marketing strategy and corporate plans, hardware technology, business strategy and plans, software, support services, and system/

product planning like was being done in Japan. IBM needed a global CA to align and integrate all of these functions for every product line.

IBM also needed to layer on an integrated, corporate-specific CA awareness to unify its top-line strategy, especially in an era of rising global competition. Our worldwide product sales were partially dependent upon competitiveness of cost per design of product hardware and how soon those were made available for manufacturing and sale.

The most important issue was Japan-specific, because their model had very promising characteristics that were truly prerequisite for growth and competition. The Japanese represented a unique and unparalleled combination of industry, government, and university focus, with computers as a national goal. In addition, they commanded significant resources and maintained a fast pace of continuous technological improvements and progress to achieve it. In short, Japan had what it took to challenge IBM. And it was our job to predict what they were going to do.

Our initial effort first required that we coordinate with the other CA operations. In addition, we needed to develop extensive data-bank and automatic search methods, hard copy file, and application of regression programs for prediction purposes. We needed competent professionals with broad technical backgrounds, continuity of CA operations, and detailed familiarity with internal programs and predictions. What we needed most were dedicated people, ready to roll up their sleeves—personnel who were both detail oriented and trained in CA operations and methods. The problem was, very few employees of the company were able to do what we did.

In response to this growing need, I was asked, along with Bob Avgherinos of IBM United Kingdom, to write a proposal to senior IBM corporate executives recommending the establishment of a Competitive Analysis Council. This would be designed to bring together, within IBM, all of the operations necessary to highlight corporate analysis, and concentrate on the Japanese corporate manufacturers' technology. Our proposal was accepted, and John Mangini of IBM Corporate was appointed to run the council. I was asked to assist in that endeavor on a worldwide basis.

We designed our training program to first develop working knowledge in the key areas listed below and then concluded with the successful passage of a final competitive technology proficiency test.

1. ~25 technology areas (modules, cards, PCBs, semiconductors, etc.)

2. ~35 technical parameters

3. Box level packaging (small systems and I/O, central processing units, memory)

4. Report generation

5. Hot line/flash operations

6. Current competitive technology, status-needs-sensitivity

7. Market and business status

8. Data collection methods and sources (periodicals, trade shows, etc.)

9. Key companies

10. Forecasting methods

11. Hardware analysis methods

This organization and training was put into place in 1973 by corporate executive order. Our job was to make it happen.

DON FRANCK

SYSTEMS PRODUCT DIVISION
Department F31 – Endicott
Extension 4061 – 7A38

March 6, 1973

Memorandum to: Mr. T. Papes
Subject: Competitive Technology Analysis
Reference: R.C. Avgherinos and D. Franck's memo of 1/19/73,
                   to you

I've had an opportunity to review with Don Franck the proposal
he and Bob Avgherinos made to you in the reference memorandum.

I support the proposal and recommend that we move forward as they
have recommended. I believe of special importance are the inputs
from Japan. To show my support, I am prepared to work out with
Ed Hofler a suitable arrangement that will assure us technology
assessments from the Japan Laboratory. If this requires funding,
as outlined in the proposal, I will find a way to handle. With
the funding issue out of the way, I believe that the overall
Competitive Analysis coordination with SPD and Group can be
handled by means such as a CA Council.

I just wanted you to know that I feel strongly enough about the
subject that I'll handle the matter with the Japan Lab and with
Don Franck's assistance see that the competitive information from
Japan is fed into all appropriate areas within SPD.

If you and Jerry Haddad agree, we'll move ahead on this basis.

J. F. Keffer

JFK/hcl

cc: Mr. J.A. Haddad
        Mr. R.V. McFadden

DEEP BLUE

IBM

Date:	June 27, 1973
From Location:	SPD Endicott
US Mail Address:	
Dept & Bldg:	U13 040-2
Tieline & Tel Ext:	1270

Subject: Japanese CA

Reference:

To: Mr. J. Mangini

You have asked me to propose a specific plan to help
establish technical competence for the Japanese Competitive
Analysis Group in Japan. The attached easel chart copies
represent my first pass at this.

D. R. Franck
SPD Competitive Technology Analysis
Test & Packaging Products

DRF/jvh

Attachment

cc: Mr. J. F. Keffer
Mr. R. G. Moyer
Mr. G. G. Werbizky
Mr. G. W. Whalen

CHAPTER 9

IBM Executive Presentations and Support

The 1970s was a time when I was really at the top of my game at IBM, via my exposure to worldwide corporate executives and getting as much recognition as someone who specialized in corporate espionage could possibly expect. While there's a certain advantage in working for a company so large, the right hand didn't always know what the left hand was doing, and despite the sometimes covert nature of competitive analysis, I nevertheless received the highest exposure within IBM, both at domestic and worldwide organizations.

The highest levels of corporate executives were aware and appreciative of what I was doing, and I was asked for competitive technology status and corporate reports regarding various computer companies and technologies on a regular basis. During the early 1970s, I made more than sixty competitive presentations to IBM presidents, division presidents, and executives. In 1979, I alone covered seven major trade shows in Europe, Japan, and the United States. Interest in the competition was quite high within IBM, and I was riding the wave.

We also established a corporate hotline to answer questions from various IBM worldwide locations. I made many high-level presentations specifically covering Japanese technology comparisons, and between 1966 and 1985 I delivered nearly 200 corporate technical evaluations and reports analyzing the competition. (See detail beginning on page 120 .)

Among IBM executives, the major concern was the growth of IBM based on sales of IBM equipment versus the timing, capability, and sales of competitive machines. Most likely, it had begun with Mr. Watson's interest in the CDC 6600 and our subsequent study of that product as detailed in Chapter 3, but there was no question how interest had spiraled since then.

My principal focus and area of expertise was the technology used in competitor machines. This required continual detailed analysis and study of the competition's equipment, which necessitated determining the technologies and quantities of materials they used, the sources of their technology, and the costs and reliability of that same technology.

I also had to examine other important issues, such as the financial ability of those competitors to survive, manufacture, market, and service their products. IBM's competitiveness, given its high operating costs, required very advanced strategic investments in technology in a timely matter and huge volumes of products to write off the worldwide investments mandated.

We accomplished this by using assets either buried in the IBM product development or technology areas to gather the data and assure that executives knew how to interpret the comparisons and forecasts. In the early 1970s alone, there were probably more than fifty people either directly or indirectly involved in competitive analysis scattered around the company, not including the IBM Data Processing Headquarters and the IBM World Trade Corporation staff. I was fortunate enough to be involved, and helped structure the competitive analysis efforts around the company and world with the support of my local, division, and corporate headquarters management.

I also was particularly pleased to receive letters of support from various people, both inside and outside IBM. One example is a letter of appreciation from Gordon Oehler, director of the CIA Scientific and Weapons Research Department; another is the acceptance letter from Tse-yun Feng, when I was made chairman of the IEEE Computer Packaging Committee. This position was most helpful to me, as it enabled me to contact employees at other companies who would help me with my competitive analysis work.

CHAPTER 10

Bill Gates, the Rise of the Personal Computer and the Evolution of IBM into Services and Software.

Like almost everyone else in the computer business, in the late 1970s and early 1980s IBM was deeply interested in the development of the PC. One didn't have to be an expert to see the possibility of a potentially huge volume and sales potential of that market for millions of new customers.

Unfortunately, IBM's existing technologies and packaging, though successful, were not cost competitive for this new market, despite the fact that those technologies were very successful in the mainframe computer business. The difference between the new PC and the mainframe was mostly cost, since the number of personal computer circuits required was quite low in comparison to those used in mainframe computers.

The PC market was still in its infancy and had yet to really develop. IBM did have the Series 1 computer, but it was costly and not well received. Our internal technology was just too expensive for the burgeoning PC market. Aware that the company was poorly positioned to exploit this opportunity, IBM began to internally explore alternatives. One approach was to look at the possibility of building a PC entirely with non-IBM parts.

It was certainly possible to buy, from the merchant semiconductor market, the transistor-transistor logic (TTL) and Intel 8088 4.77 MHZ processor devices to build a PC, as well as the rest of the packaging and electronics. But the notion of purchasing parts from outside the IBM empire caused much political infighting and internal conflict at the company.

In short, using internal IBM technology was not competitive for the PC product compared to outside-purchased technology. I had many conversations with Joe Sarubbi, who was one of the key project engineers working for Bill Lowe who headed the PC program in Boca Raton, Florida. These made it clear that in addition to the intrinsic costs of the existing technologies that IBM used for other products, if a component was bought from an existing IBM manufacturing facility, there was always a tax from that IBM manufacturing site to an IBM buying site.

As counterintuitive as interdivisional taxation might seem, it's not that uncommon in very large organizations. In this case, the practice exacerbated an already nagging problem with cost control. If an IBM product manufacturing location was buying parts from a non-local in-house IBM source, that source charged a tax on those parts to the in-house buyer, which increased manufacturing costs by at least 10 percent to 30 percent. These internal costs, added to the technologies' cost, would make the product price much too high for the market. For instance, the IBM 5100, an earlier version of the PC that IBM designed, was not successful using internal technology and costs, so IBM decided to use outside technology for its personal computer.

But the decision did not always go down well. Our internal technology groups were accustomed to having a lock on manufacturing parts. Although they certainly saw the value and wanted to capture the sales volume expected for the PC, they refused to recognize that to use IBM's internal technology and manufacturing would produce a machine far too expensive and beyond the reach of most customers. On the other hand, IBM PC product management understood that and wanted to buy the parts from outside of IBM. Yet, in the end, PC management prevailed.

It was eventually decided that the logic design and electronics were to be built from largely non-IBM sources. The end product turned out to be very low in price and very successful. It was released as the IBM PC product on August 12, 1981. Just over a year later, on January 3, 1983, the IBM PC was awarded the *Time* magazine "Man (Machine) of the Year" award.[1]

At this time, I provided outside and competitor technology information that was used by many divisions within IBM. There was particular interest in the electronic packaging technology that was so critical in development of the PC product information. I had many discussions with PC engineers and visited Boca Raton to discuss outside capability and sourcing. The rise of the PC was the beginning of the end of the traditional mainframe computer business because of

1   Magazine cover image published by Listal.com, accessed 10-11-2014, http://www.listal.com/list/time-magazines-person-year.

the growing use of new complementary metal-oxide semiconductor (CMOS) technology to replace the conventional bipolar circuits like TTL, Schottkey transistor-transistor logic (STTL), and emitter-coupled logic (ECL) used in the mainframe business. The use of CMOS and similar circuits and devices eventually offered better cost and performance for a wide range of products.

Yet one of those conversations stands out in my mind. In 1980, I was called down to IBM Corporate to sit in on a four-person meeting with a man named Bill Gates. He was being interviewed for a job designing an operating system for the IBM PC. IBM elected to go ahead with Gates, who agreed to design the operating system at a very low cost. In the process, IBM gave Gates the rights to the disk operating system for his own use. It may have been a critical mistake. For that was the kickstart that launched what would become the Microsoft Corporation. Within ten years, Microsoft would successfully challenge IBM with its revolutionary Windows system in a software rivalry that was raging by 1990. A real David-and-Goliath story if ever there was one.

My contacts at the executive level were very capable and aware of industry opinions on various issues. But later observers of that very competitive time have characterized IBM as a divided company whose leadership—a "Big Gray Cloud of Managers"—was out of touch with the world and its demands.[2]

The advent of advanced CMOS devices would eventually affect the hardwire technology advances IBM had created. IBM responded successfully by focusing on software and services, and by eventually selling off and closing the internal focus on hardware technology. The newly named Z systems for mainframes ultimately replaced the older names and certainly indicated the importance of mainframe revenue for IBM.

---

2   Paul Carroll, *Big Blues: The Unmaking of IBM* (New York: Three Rivers Press, 1993), 267.

CHAPTER 11

IBM's Analysis of Russian Computer Technology for the CIA

As much as I enjoyed what I was doing for IBM, my work was about to take an even more serious turn. In late 1982, I received a call from Dick Immershein, who was head of Competitive Analysis for Products at Data Processing Headquarters in Armonk, New York (then the corporate office). He asked about Russian computer technology. Other than seeing a few displays at the Hannover Fair in Germany, I had no real exposure to, or knowledge of, that technology, but I believed that with further acquaintance with it, I could compare it with the rest of the world's computer technology.

Shortly thereafter, I was called to Nick Katzenbach's office in Armonk. Mr. Katzenbach was the lead IBM attorney and had previously served as the United States Attorney General during John F. Kennedy's and Lyndon Johnson's administrations during the early 1960s. He joined IBM in 1969, where he is perhaps best known for his work on the lengthy antitrust case filed by the Department of Justice seeking the breakup of IBM. He and fellow attorney Thomas Barr led the IBM case for thirteen years, until the government dropped it in 1982.[3]

---

3   Source: Wikipedia, http://en.wikipedia.org/wiki/Nicholas_Katzenbach, accessed 11-11-2014.

At that initial meeting in Armonk, there were several people in the room. I was asked again if I could help answer the CIA's question about the current state of Russian computer technology, and I said perhaps, if I could get access to their data. Mr. Katzenbach then assigned me, along with an IBM lawyer, to go to Washington, D.C., and interview with the CIA for the assignment. Yet again, I was mindful of my experiences during the Cold War. It was a big assignment and carried a lot of responsibility, and I was only too happy to take it on.

We traveled to Washington and met at the Department of Commerce Building with the CIA to discuss the project. When I said I needed Russian computer and technology data to perform an analysis, the CIA representative told me they had filing cabinets full of technical information and some defectors who might supply the necessary information.

I went by myself to CIA headquarters to look over the hard copy files. Extracting the information would require considerable time and review. Over several visits, I was able to put together the information I needed to portray and forecast Russian computer and technology status for the next ten to twenty years in comparison with the rest of the world's computer technology. I was also very impressed with the CIA itself—from the stars on the wall memorializing their lost agents to the caliber of the people. I thought we were in good and safe hands given the skills and patriotism of these people, and was glad to have a part in their operations, however small.

Social, economic, business, political, and a multiplicity of other factors all have an effect on the potential for technology introduction, and all of these were important for the evaluation of Russian technology as compared with other countries around the globe.

My work on the status of the Soviet information technology preceded the era of Gorbachev and détente, and reflected the conditions at the height of the Cold War. At that time, data and observations suggested an economic system that rewarded production quotas regardless of whether the products were what the people wanted, whether the products worked, or whether the products got to where they were supposed to be on time.

The system also penalized criticism that would normally correct these same problems, as well as the kind of individual initiative that could provide leadership. Without a profit-based system that responded to a population's requirements rather than the communist ruling-class decisions, there was no forced efficiency and response. Therefore, Soviet enterprises survived economically by edict.

By contrast, the United States in this era was characterized by a free enterprise economy with new and major computer system offerings incorporating a significant technology change approximately every five to seven years. The major part of the mainframe computer market was confined to a small number of companies with massive marketing, production, and reliability skills that employed advanced technology. Their products had become a de facto standard worldwide.

Based on what we found out, there could be little expected in natural technology improvement or incentive in the Soviet system, unless the initiative was political. One-party control, without the ability to have multiple candidates for public office, merely perpetuated the ruling class and secured the entrenchment of inferior leaders and policies that were probably pervasive. The single exception was in the area of armament, where outside competition influenced the Soviets to be competitive. And they were largely forced to buy, steal, or copy existing non-Soviet technology to do that.

Also, without a system of accountability, and with a philosophy that dictated the "end justifies the means," there was little concern about ordinary and ethical business methods. Unlike the West, the Soviets had considerable difficulty forming long-term business relationships with other companies or the advantage of networking.

The data did seem to indicate that "détente" was a benefit technically—primarily for the Soviets because it meant they could legitimately try to obtain worldwide technology or equipment that they had little hope of developing successfully on their own. But at the same time, we found many examples of serious deficiencies in printed circuit manufacturing skill and technology, such as in dry film materials, drilling machines, testers, and other evidence. Their printed circuit conductor line width controls of one line per channel and 10 to 15 mils width were years behind Western and Japanese standards.

In addition, they had serious problems with yield, worker discontent, worker productivity and absenteeism, water and power, and the environment (such as the impact on livestock and the public caused by printed circuit etching effluent dumped in the countryside). Some Eastern Bloc countries with somewhat less-rigid bureaucracies had better abilities to improve upon their products and technology, but only to the point where progress began to intrude upon centralized communist economic theory, dogma, and control.

In short, it didn't appear their system could reasonably be expected to compete in high and new applied technology areas. Therefore, they had to acquire these from outside sources. Thus, I concluded after I finished my evaluation, the CIA's worry about Russian computer technology was unfounded, and the real industrial threat in the computer and technology area was from the Japanese computer manufacturers.

The JCMs had all the technological skill of their American counterparts with the added advantage of working within selected government programs that set national priorities and financing and established programs for the computer industry as a top priority. The three major computer companies that were of concern in this analysis were Nippon Electronics Corporation (NEC), Fujitsu, and Hitachi. They were at the forefront of the direct worldwide challenge to IBM, then the established leader.

The computer or information technology industry had many dimensions that led to Japanese strengths. Rather than requiring raw materials, this sector required only a people-based resource—a workforce that was educated, cooperative, and homogeneous. Japan was also without border or culture problems and very much aware that it must export to survive. The people worked in a cooperative, highly motivated manner, possibly a result of a crowded environment and small land mass.

By the 1970s, quality was of extreme importance to the Japanese. Cost was low due to automation and high employee productivity, and the companies were vertically integrated with the added benefit of selling components and technology on the open market, which permitted an expanded volume base to further reduce costs.

NEC offered computer hardware and software that was incompatible with IBM software. It also had a more advanced multi-chip module base technically superior to that of its competitors, Fujitsu and Hitachi (Fujitsu and Hitachi had elected to go with compatible IBM software). The general rate of technological progress and improvement in Japan had been extraordinary in all technical areas. I believe they were the world leader in shipping applied science in products across the electronic spectrum.

There was significant and continued cooperation among the national Japanese companies, the MITI, and the university system, with an emphasis on technology as applied to products that could be exported. The JCMs and Japanese organizations like the Japan Institute for Promotion of Digital Economy and Community and the Japan External Trade Organization collected, tracked, and projected technology trends the world over.

Ultimately, the curves I portrayed in my results showed the JCMs and U.S. computer manufacturers versus the Russian Ryad Series, and it was clear the Russians were, and would continue to be, well behind the West.

Methodology

My report and analysis started with a fundamental technical assumption that knowing the past could help predict the future and, barring quantum jumps, would be within a reasonable range of accuracy based on year of interest. This top-down methodology has been the basis for my IBM projections of competition in the area of my expertise for twenty years. It had proven to be relatively accurate and easily able to accommodate raw data for updates.

The most difficult assignment is to start from scratch and try to gather existing data in new areas not previously examined, with the goal of forming some accurate historical substance in the database. Most important is to select those technical parameters of first order effect that can be easily gathered and which characterize the technology and its performance. On occasion, new parameters may be more important and old ones less important, and so parameter selection is a dynamically evaluated chore. Also, continuity of judgment and database accuracy is extremely important.

Each parameter, while of key significance, must also be put into an accurate time frame, establishing its introduction and use. It is difficult and very important to separate academic or company or national publicity from real use and the availability of hardware and technology. As I indicated before, the first customer shipment date of the system or product shipped to a customer actually using the technology is defined as the real availability date. This study does not look at technology availability, per se; it uses as a base foundation the introduction of technology in shipped systems.

This means that to use a technology in a product that first shipped in 1985, the work on the technology, including design, testing, sample parts, and manufacturability, must have preceded the product use by possibly five to seven years, at least in the computer business. Unique technology development projections may be done without regard to application, and these may precede their actual use.

Commercial uniprocessors were selected as the base of judgment for my evaluation, and the computer's performance in millions of instructions per second (MIPS) was based on the cost performance and high-performance computer product spectrum. It is possible, and there is significant industry example, to build much higher performance systems using relatively simple technology. For instance, because of machine architecture and parallelism, the design of array processors using simple and old technology can have much higher performance than a commercial uniprocessor design using more advanced technology on certain problems. But array processors are used in unique applications.

In addition, floating point processors attached to a commercial system can have selective and extraordinary performance improvements, but these anomalies are clearly designed for a special class of problems. Machines like the Cray-1 were predominantly designed for large matrix problems such as seismic, weather, nuclear, or cryptographic jobs. This kind of computer structure using advanced commercial technology could, of course, be much faster than the same machine using simple technology. Or, in reverse, because of machine design and architecture, and with simple technology, it could operate much faster on some problems than any commercial uniprocessor for business applications that may be using more complex technology.

From a competitive analysis point of view then, the ultimate value is to be able to predict in the future, five to ten years and beyond, what the natural trends will be for the various technologies, industries, companies, and countries under consideration, and, based on those conditions, make technical investments and set priorities policy that will assist in remaining competitive for sometimes years to come. Once natural directions are set, from a top-down predictive viewpoint, it is possible to arrive at technology requirements and parameter specifications based on a bottom-up technology evaluation that relates product needs in the context of technological capabilities.

This exercise is to find the leverage points, from a technical point of view, that permit cost and performance goals to be met by the final product. There are usually numerous alternatives to arriving at an end product point, and it is critically important to exercise the technical alternatives and choices on how best to get there.

There was an upcoming and fast-improving performance range of small computers using CMOS, gate arrays, microprocessors, and similar new technologies, that were in a special but growing performance class of systems as apart from that of large commercial mainframes. There is some risk that extrapolations may be interpreted to mean that those particular parameter requirements may always be required in order to achieve the system's performance, and this is not always the case.

For example, the Fujitsu 380 and Hitachi 280H both used significantly less module technology (single-chip modules and multi-chip modules) than the IBM 3081, but had approximately the same performance. That said, the technical base in the 3081 should permit much more volume manufacturing capability and more technology extendibility and ultimately lead to far higher machine performance capability at a lower cost. In addition, there are other considerations, such as reliability, cost, and volume manufacturability.

Finally, not all parameters always coexist, and in fact may mitigate against each other. We tend to assume that because all parameters are plotted separately that they are therefore independent, when in fact they are mostly interdependent.

In considering the environment of these three major areas of my study, I concluded that the Soviets would fall farther and farther behind if they did not have access to foreign technology for their computer industry, especially without détente. It may even have been a factor in the subsequent collapse of their system. They could, however, purchase the components and technology from the West, unless they were made inaccessible.

Japan was obviously a superior source for all the technology the Russians would need. I suspected much of their technology was already available to them to some extent through Finnish, Indian, or other indirect sources. The French had also been relatively accommodating in supplying technology and equipment. But left on their own, the Soviets, without Western help or a change in their system, would not continue to have viable production, performance, or reliability capability in the commercial high-performance or cost-performance uniprocessor computer area—although their theoretical science was probably adequate and good.

In my assessment, I believed that they could, however, certainly be able to build a limited number of large, very high-performance special-purpose parallel machines with relatively primitive and available technology. This was the status prior to détente.

In brief, these were my conclusions:

Soviet Status – High-Performance Machines

1. If the Soviets were to build high-performance systems, they would have to do so using their own primitive technology or acquire technology or CPUs elsewhere for future products/usage.

2. There would likely be a serious negative reliability effect and system downtime, if the choice was to use older, primitive technology.

3. Multiprocessor versions of older hardware would have better performance than uniprocessors. Special high-performance array processors could be built out of primitive technology.

4. The Soviet ability to manufacture and service in quantity was believed to be much less than that of the West and Japan.

5. Logic and packaging technology were seriously weak; this was probably the case with memory as well.

6. There was a serious and difficult technology hurdle in bridging from 4.5 MIPS uniprocessors to the 40-MIPS machine forecast for 1990, with incremental performance machines required along the way.

Soviet Status – Cost-Performance Machines

- Cost-performance machines were much easier to attain with primitive technology than high-performance machines.

- Technology through 1982 was adequate to obtain CPU cost-performance goals, though somewhat later than the West. Growth in performance to 12 MIPS in 1990 would require some new technology to be developed.

- Multiprocessor computer versions of existing Soviet hardware could meet CPU performance objectives. Special processors (array and floating point processors) would help CPU performance for special job streams.

- The Soviet ability to manufacture and service in quantity was believed to be much less than in the West and in Japan.

- I made some derating of the effect of the Russian technology deficiency due to the lesser need for technology in some areas (1979 to 1990).

Additional technical findings and observations about Soviet information technology prior to détente are summarized in Appendix 2 and 3.

In my conclusions, I told the CIA that the Soviets under communism were not competitive with Western computer technology, particularly not with IBM and the JCMs, for commercial computer technology, and that they would not be competitive in the foreseeable future.

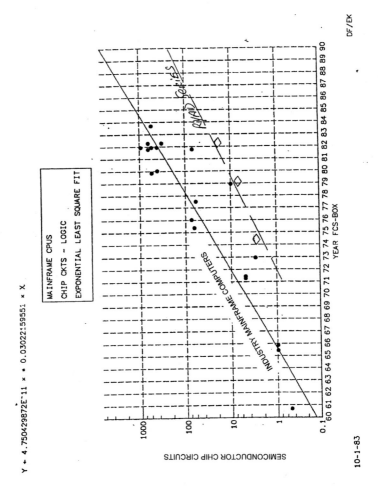

Those at the CIA seemed more than pleased with my results. Not long afterward Patrick Toole, then president of the Systems Technology Division, and myself received the following letter of appreciation. But while there were changes coming up in my career at IBM, it wasn't the last I'd hear from the CIA.

Central Intelligence Agency

Washington, D.C. 20505

฿฿ 1994

Mr. Patrick Toole
President,
IBM Systems Technology Division
1701 North Street
Endicott, NY   14760

Dear Mr. Toole:

I would like to express my appreciation to you for permitting Mr. Donald Franck to participate in a recent technical study for my organization. We are constantly seeking the best measures of effectiveness for many critical technologies. Mr. Franck's contribution on electronics and packaging has provided us with the benefit of his knowledge and experience to quantify and interpret these areas of computer technology. Please convey my appreciation to Mr. Franck for an excellent technical contribution to our study.

Sincerely,

Gordon C. Oehler
Director
Scientific and Weapons Research

cc: Mr. Donald Franck
    STD/Endicott

CHAPTER 12

The CMOS *versus Bipolar Semiconductor Study*

A few years before my retirement as a senior engineer from IBM in 1987, I asked to be transferred from the electronic packaging area in Endicott into the Endicott Glendale Product Development Lab. This was in the Computer Development Competitive Analysis area under Tom Dougherty and Bill Virun. The transfer gave me a much closer understanding of the impact of technology on the cost and performance of the system's mainframe products as it impacted product costs.

Most of the technologies being used for the IBM cost and performance products at that time used subsets of the earlier SLT/monolithic semiconductor technology (MST) and follow-on technologies that used bipolar circuits. I was concerned that the alternative choice of using much denser but slower and fewer CMOS circuits to design a product might provide a possible advantage over the bipolar circuit and chip choice that was currently being used in mainframes. CMOS is the semiconductor technology used in most of today's computer microchips and in many other products and PCs.

Here some further explanation may be helpful. An early bipolar transistor circuit basically had three terminals—a base, a collector, and an emitter. Computer logic or memory can be performed using many semiconductor chips with this kind of device. By comparison, the CMOS device has many more circuits than a bipolar device, and is usually slower, with less power per circuit. For this reason, the CMOS device is used for memory, microprocessors, and other applications where low cost, low power, and high density is crucial for the final application. Hence, their popularity in today's "personal" electronics market.

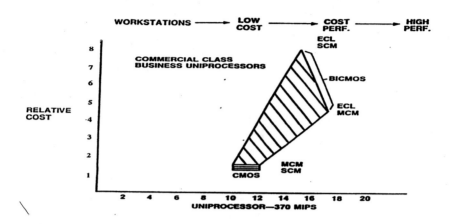

After completing my study in 1987, my conclusions of those competing technology options showed the following results:

- Processor and memory design and architecture can affect performance results significantly.

- A twenty-five- to thirty-nanosecond computer CPU machine cycle at the time may be a cycle time performance barrier for a typical office environment for complementary CMOS-based single-chip or multi-chip designs.

- Multi-chip processor performance is not limited for the cases assumed and will permit faster than fifteen-nanosecond cycle times and 15- to 17-MIPS machines.

- A single-chip module implementation is cheaper when only a "few" chips are in the system.

- A multi-chip module implementation is cheaper when there are "many" chips in the system, and it permits a performance advantage as well.

The above curves suggest that the eventual abandonment of ECL bipolar devices would occur because the cost performance advantage of very dense but slower CMOS devices would prevail. And once again, my predictions proved correct.

A further trend goes far beyond the above study, and that is the increasing capability of CMOS and other semiconductor devices to change the cost and performance of the mainframe and other product business.

In 1965, Dr. Gordon Moore of the INTEL Corporation forecasted that semiconductor chip circuits would exponentially double every ten years. In 1975, he revised that to indicate it would double every two years. Dr. Michio Kaku forecasted that the technology is continually improving, but the semiconductor future may be 3D, optical, or protein chips that would replace devices in the post-silicon era. My own empirical extrapolation of the chip circuits indicates one million to possibly ten million may be on the future horizon.

CHAPTER 13

After IBM

During early June 1987, while I was still a senior engineer with IBM, I met my friend Ray Rinne at a party at Quaker Lake, Pennsylvania, where Ray had a summer home (and where we have a home today). Ray had taken a position as a senior executive at DuPont after retiring from IBM's East Fishkill headquarters.

At that time, IBM had an early retirement offer on the table for some employees and Ray encouraged me to take it. It consisted of adding five years to your age and five years to your years with IBM. At that point, I had thirty-one years with the company and I was fifty-three years old. This gave me thirty-six years with IBM and an effective age of fifty-eight years. IBM also offered to bring me back on a contract basis. In addition, Ray offered me a consulting contract with DuPont to do competitive analysis and technology forecasting. I negotiated a four-year no-cut contract with DuPont for a tidy sum and decided to accept the IBM retirement offer.

By setting up an LLC consulting company, I was able to submit reports and evaluate technology for DuPont in my spare time as well as fulfill my contractual obligations to IBM. During this same period I was asked by Rudy Lawson, the president of the Universal Instrument Corporation (UIC), to do some consulting in electronic packaging for him. UIC was a very successful company that built automation equipment for the assembly of electronic packages. It was founded in the Binghamton, New York area, and was then owned by the Dover Corporation, a publicly traded company. When I finished my assignment with UIC, I was asked to join Dover Electronics, which was run by Ron Budacz.

At the time, Dover was managing a demonstration manufacturing line to show UIC customers how their automation equipment worked (Dover was a division of UIC at that time). Since I still had an ongoing contract with DuPont, I was able to keep that and then sold my small consulting company to Dover and received a nice employment contract along with the title of president of one of their consulting divisions called Empire Planning. I was also the VP of technology for Dover Electronics, reporting to Ron Budacz, then division president.

Dover maintained several formal relationships with IBM at the time. It worked on a contract with IBM for manufacturing metallization patterns of a ceramic substrate, which they called the MC Program. Dover also had an IBM contract with East Fishkill for the lamination of multilayer substrates. When customized with wiring patterns, these substrates were later fired in a curing furnace to become a multilayer, multi-chip stack of ceramic. This was the multi-chip multilayer carrier for the semiconductors used in the most advanced of IBM's multi-chip (100 chips) thermal conductor module programs used in large high-performance commercial computer systems.

This was an exciting time for Dover Electronics and me personally. Ron, a retired colonel, was an aggressive businessman who saw that, rather than just being a demonstration area for UIC automation equipment, there was great opportunity to grow that business into a national assembly services contract for large corporations. As a result, the emphasis changed from a demonstration services line for UIC equipment to a growing assembly company with worldwide potential. While Dover's electronics growth was large, the profit margins were small in comparison to those in the rest of the Dover Corporation, where the opposite was true.

Yet from the corporate point of view, that presented some problems. The more Dover Electronics' sales volume grew, the more negatively it began to affect the appearance of the very profitable Dover Corporation (due to its low profit margins). During this period, I advised on technology aspects and requirements for Dover Electronics, which was eventually renamed Dovatron and spun off from the Dover Corporation as a separate, publicly-traded company.

Dovatron then stood on its own in terms of sales and earnings, and I was very actively looking for acquisitions for Dovatron. In particular, I had personal contact with a major customer of Dover Electronics, Harry Horn, who was a vice president at a company called Standard Microsystems (SMC) and who would ultimately become a close friend. SMC had sizeable international sales of various telecommunication products and was using a division of the Western Digital Company located in Cork, Ireland, to manufacture their products for the European market.

Unfortunately, Western Digital was downsizing at the time and wanted to get out of their manufacturing operation in Ireland. Dr. Bob Elfant was a senior executive at Western Digital at the time, and I knew him reasonably well from our IBM days. I also knew that when companies located in Ireland, they received many grants and financial incentives from the Irish government, but if a company closed, the financial penalties could be severe.

My problem was to determine the volume of international sales for SMC that would justify the business case for an acquisition by Dover Electronics before we were spun off. It took some time to determine the viability since there was some confusion as to what parts overseas were being assembled and in what volume. But with Bob Egan's sales information support, it became clear that the manufacturing volume justified a purchase. The only holdup was the price. In considering the large financial exposure that Western Digital had with the Irish government, I decided that we should offer $1 million and no more for all operations, equipment, and personnel at the Cork facility. The Western Digital assignee at the Cork operation was Dermott O'Flanagan, and he was supposed to try to negotiate the price.

As Dermott, Rich Kenehan (the controller at Dover Electronics at the time), and I were going through security at the Broome County Airport in Binghamton, New York, Dermott insisted that the price had to be a lot higher than $1 million. Hearing that, I simply turned around and started to leave the airport, since I didn't want to offer more. It was with some trepidation that I did so. I secretly believed the Cork operation was worth more than $1 million, but I didn't want to play that card. Fortunately, Dermott got my point. He ran after me and said he would go along with the million-dollar offer. And Dover Corporation and Ron Budacz accepted the deal.

I was delighted my ploy had worked, but I still had to get a financial commitment from SMC for production. But thanks to Harry Horn, I was able to get a purchase order in hand for $16 million to confirm their financial commitment. It was not long afterward that the Dover board of directors decided that Dover Electronics should be spun off from Dover itself and that the new company was to be called Dovatron.

During my years at Dovatron, I continued to look for suitable acquisition candidates, in addition to my VP of technology responsibilities. One that came to my attention was a company called the Multek Corporation, which was located in the Los Angeles area. This organization manufactured large, very complex printed circuits, including standard FR4 materials in addition to Teflon or complex polyimide printed circuit materials. As I recall, their sales were in the $30 million range, but their earnings were about $12 million. That was hugely different from any other printed circuit board (PCB) company I had ever looked at, since earnings were so low in those companies due to their production costs.

Dovatron was now a public company with relatively low earnings, so I took the earnings from Multek and applied them to the Dovatron share price to show my boss, Ron Budacz, what the benefits would be to the price of Dovatron shares. I knew if we could do it, Dovatron's share price would explode. The only issue was what to pay for Multek.

Ron came to work one morning and told me he had a dream about what to pay for Multek. I asked what that was, and he said $20 million. I told him in no uncertain terms that price was a deal-killer. Why would the owner ever agree to such a low price, based on his earnings? Unconvinced, Ron called the owner, and sure enough, the owner promptly hung up on him. Later on, we finally closed the deal for about $50 million and it was still a bargain. Just as I'd forecasted, the price of Dovatron shares went through the roof as a result.

During these years, I traveled worldwide with Ron. One time I took him to visit Kazuo Inamori, then president of Kyocera Ceramics, located in Kagoshima, Japan. Inamori had become one of the most successful Japanese entrepreneurs and businessmen, and he was a very competent executive. He was also a black belt. We were interested in discussing the potential for our metallized ceramic equipment located in our buildings (which was originally a contract with IBM).

During the time with Dovatron and Dover Electronics, I had further contact with the CIA, which expressed interest in certain assignments in the Middle East. Fortunately, I was able to help them on that project, which was to determine the status of Gaddafi's work on developing nuclear weapons. At various times I would talk with my CIA representatives and discuss potential views and contacts, although most of the evaluation work was done on-site in Libya by my CIA contacts, who used business cards from my company to enable them to operate there. Those details and contacts are still confidential, but suffice to say that Gaddafi and Libya terminated their work on development of a nuclear bomb.

After I retired from Dovatron in 1995, I was again called by the CIA to assist on an espionage requirement in South East Asia. Fortunately, I was able to assist on that successful and still confidential project. I must say that over the years, all my contacts with the CIA were most exciting. I found my contacts at the CIA to be very well educated, honorable, and patriotic Americans, and the CIA deserves many compliments for their work and personal risk on behalf of our country.

CHAPTER 14

Around the World on a Business Trip – Not All Work and No Play

Over a twenty-year period, I traveled throughout Europe, the Middle East, Asia, the United States, and Australia. I learned so much about other places and cultures, that even though business was always my main focus, there were many situations and sidelights that were most interesting to me. I thought I would share them with readers (these are not in any particular order of coverage, but as I recall them).

Singapore, Hong Kong, Macao, and China

On trips to Singapore, I have always marveled at the cleanliness, organization, and security of the country. It's little wonder that many first-class manufacturing companies that were very competitive on a worldwide basis were headquartered there. On my first trip, I had the good fortune to stay at Raffles Hotel, which had the "long bar" where the Singapore Sling was invented. Over many years, there were famous visitors to that bar, such as Ernest Hemingway, Rudolph Giuliani, W. Somerset Maugham, Queen Elizabeth, and many other notables.

On one subsequent trip, I was leading a Southeast Asia team visit to explore printed circuit manufacturing and assembly facilities. After breakfast at Raffles, our local manufacturing executive took us to play golf at a wonderful golf course in Malaysia, which was accessed by crossing the land bridge into that country from Singapore. We had a great day playing golf and chasing the monkeys away from stealing our golf balls on the fairways.

As I recall it, you had to be careful about chasing golf balls that went into the nearby jungle. If we hit a ball into the jungle, we just left it there since we never could be sure what danger lurked. After a day of golf, our host took us to the wonderful clubhouse for dinner. We assembled outside the clubhouse to return to Singapore at about 8 p.m. As I was getting into the back seat of our car, somehow our host drove over my foot. This was the first day of a two-week competitive analysis trip that started in Singapore and then moved on to Hong Kong, China, Macao, and Korea. Fortunately, my foot wasn't broken, but I had to use crutches for the next two weeks.

The next step on that trip was to visit Hong Kong (on my crutches) and the new territories in China. Although I had been to Hong Kong many times, I always looked forward to a visit there. Prior to the takeover by China, Hong Kong was an exciting place, and perhaps it hasn't changed much since then. We visited several printed circuit manufacturing facilities, and at one I noticed a worker at the end of the etching line, where harsh chemicals were used, loading the still-wet printed circuits onto a metal frame. He was dressed in shorts and sandals, and the chemicals were dripping on him. Later on we noticed that the plant's chemical effluent was being discharged into Hong Kong harbor, where people were fishing. I can only be thankful that awareness of safety and environmental factors has increased substantially since then.

Later, we met one of our manufacturing reps, who took us to Macao, which was Portuguese at the time, to view their manufacturing lines. For the trip to Macao, he took us on one of his two 100-foot luxury boats around Hong Kong harbor and then on to Macao. The factory we visited was very modern and had an estimated 1,000 employees, mostly young women. They were all in uniforms and were very hard working.

This particular company also sponsored sports teams and other activities for recreation. We were very impressed with their manufacturing operation. I also noticed that the chairs for employees were quite small, which I asked about. The manufacturing manager said that if a person didn't fit into the chair, they were too big, used too much air, and were slower than other employees, so they did not hire those people. Just try to get those guidelines used in American manufacturing plants.

We went on from Macao to the new territories in China and then on to South Korea. In Korea, I was able to get special approval to visit the demilitarized zone between North and South Korea. I could see firsthand from the watch towers the backwardness of North Korea. The lack of "success" of this supposed socialist paradise persists today. It stands in stark contrast to South Korea and their freedom and free enterprise, where the industriousness and work ethic of the people is well known and extraordinary. Also, the many manufacturing plants we visited in South Korea were quite modern and busy as well as being quite competitive.

Israel and Hong Kong

Although the threat of international terrorism is relatively new in the States, many other countries in the world have had to contend with it for a long time. One time, I had to fly from Los Angeles, where I had attended a trade show, to Paris and then eventually on to Hong Kong and Japan. I arrived at JFK, changed planes, and then flew on to Paris, then Israel.

At the Tel Aviv airport, all passengers were taken off the plane due to an Islamic terrorist train attack in the Balkans. A woman sitting in front of me refused to get off the plane, so an Israeli commando rammed a rifle butt into the seat next to her head and she quickly exited. The plane and passengers were then thoroughly searched. After several hours, we took off for Bombay, then went on to Bangkok and Hong Kong.

On the flight to Bombay, India, I was seated next to a man who was Muslim. We got to talking, and I asked about the Muslim religion. His reply was that it was not a religion at all but a way of life. He spoke glowingly about the Koran. I wondered at the time if our U.S. Constitution and Bill of Rights would protect a "way of life" if it were not a religion.

Upon arrival in Hong Kong, I found that I had so many traveling bags that it was hard to handle and keep track of them. I decided to buy a large suitcase, and after I had packed everything, I called the hotel porter and asked him to take the bag down to the curb to the taxi. The bag was so big he was unable to carry it, so he had to call an additional porter. When I got to the taxi, the bag was of such size that it wouldn't fit into the taxi along with me so I had to hire another taxi to carry just the bag. So much for my bag consolidation.

Japan

I took my first trip to Japan after we had justified to the IBM corporate office the need for an on-site competitive analysis group because of the threat from the Japanese computer manufacturers. Nobuo Mii, nicknamed "Nobby," invited our group—Bob Avgherinos from IBM UK; Jay Greenman from the IBM Burlington memory area; H. B. Okamoto, selected to run the IBM Japan competitive study area; John Mangini, assigned by the IBM corporate office to head up the first Competitive Analysis Council; and me—to go to dinner.

Nobby took us all out to a restaurant that also housed national art treasures. Our group sat down on cushions, and individual waitresses served us dinner—and what a dinner it was! Each of the fifteen or so dishes was small and very unique. We all had chopsticks with which we were largely unfamiliar, but we struggled on. I remember one dish that I chewed and chewed but could not seem to swallow. In order to not offend our host, I took a large gulp of beer and swallowed the whole thing at one time. I found out later on that it was pickled jellyfish. It was a most memorable evening. The group of us went on to visit Mount Fuji and tour around Japan, including visiting the IBM facilities.

We were all staying at the Tokyo Hilton, which was in the Akasaka area, and not a far walk from the Sanno Hotel where General MacArthur had his headquarters. The Sanno Hotel was used by many companies' executives and officers of the U.S. military. It was my first try at Mongolian barbecue, shabu, and tempura prepared by Japanese chefs. The property that the Sanno occupied was so valuable that the Japanese government subsequently bought the property and made another site available for the hotel.

On another occasion, upon my arrival in Japan, I took a taxi to the Tokyo Hilton (which later on became the Capital Tokyo) to meet a large gathering of senior IBM executives from the United States, Japan, and Europe. After my presentation of another competitive technology analysis report, at the end of the day, a number of these executives met in the hotel bar for a short time and then we all left to take the elevators to our rooms.

The elevator car was full, so one of the executives remained in the lobby to catch the next elevator. After the elevator doors closed, two very attractive young girls ran up and each took an arm of the gentleman still waiting for the elevator. When the elevator doors opened, it was still full of the same group who had just left (apparently, someone had pushed the wrong button and the elevator had gone down instead of up). Of course, when the elevator doors opened, all the executives saw the lone man, now with the two girls attached. He must have been very embarrassed. I don't know if he was able to keep his job after that exposure, since IBM was a very strict company.

Taiwan

I arrived in Taiwan in the early evening for a technical conference. After checking in at the large hotel and unpacking, I noticed that the blazer I had brought was soiled, so I called the front desk and asked if they could clean it. Shortly, a porter arrived at my room and took the coat with him, saying that it would be cleaned by the next morning.

The next morning a porter delivered the cleaned coat. I then tried on the coat and found that it had shrunk and that my sleeves were now at least six inches too short. I complained to the porter, and he then called the hotel manager, who soon arrived at my room. He was very apologetic and said that they would replace the coat. He then had a tailor at the local haberdashery shop measure me in the hotel room for a replacement. They delivered a new duplicate cashmere coat that evening, which I tried on immediately. It was beautiful and perfect and at no cost.

Several weeks later I returned home, unpacked, and put the new coat into a closet. Lo and behold, I found my original coat still in the closet. However, a coat belonging to my son, who was then twelve years old, was missing. I had mistakenly taken the wrong coat when I left for Taiwan, and that was the coat that had been "shrunk" by the hotel cleaners.

The United Kingdom and Germany

On another trip for IBM competitive analysis, I had to attend the Electronica trade show in Munich, Germany. Knowing I had to spend some time in Europe, I took the occasion beforehand to play golf with some of my friends who play first-class courses around the world every two years. This time we played at many UK courses, including the old course at St. Andrews, Scotland. While I am not a great golfer, at one time I was able to shoot a 76 at that course.

During the traveling between courses and hotels across Scotland and England, we usually ate dinner at the boarding house or small hotel where we stayed. While at one dinner, I bit into something hard and thought I had broken a tooth and lost an expensive gold cap in the process. We were not able to find the cap at that time, so I told the proprietor that I would pay $50 if someone could find the cap. The next day, I called the restaurant to see if they had found the cap. They had gone through all the garbage, but no luck. (When I eventually got home and went to my dentist and told him what happened, he said, "Open up." He then told me that I did not lose a cap but had merely bitten into something hard. I often think of that incident with some embarrassment.)

Several days later, I left our golf group to complete my IBM competitive analysis mission in Europe. I arrived in Munich on a Friday and stayed at the Platzl Hotel near the Hofbräuhaus, a large historic bar the World War 2 Germans and Nazis apparently frequented. I was told that Hitler also had visited there. The waitresses delivered three huge flasks of beer in each hand. That took real strength.

The Electronica trade show had many exhibits that I visited to gather competitive information. Since they were exhibitors, I was able to view Russian computer science, but it was very limited and they were very close-mouthed about anything technical. Later on, when I did the study for the CIA, I was only able to pass on limited Soviet technology information from this source.

While in Munich, I also visited the Olympic Games location where the radical Islamists killed members of the Israeli wrestling team. I was called on the following Sunday by Frank Cummisky, who was head of IBM World Trade Operations in Europe at the time, and told that they had changed the date of my presentation to all the country presidents and I had to get to Paris headquarters a day earlier than planned. So I checked out of my hotel and it was on to Paris.

France

I love Paris, having been there many times, and I especially looked forward to that portion of my trip. Usually, my meetings were at the IBM Rue du Retiro executive offices. I made my competitive analysis presentation to all the country presidents, and after some follow-up questions, was left on my own for several days before returning home. I took the occasion to visit Harry's New York Bar, which was near the Intercontinental Hotel where I usually stayed. I had been to Harry's many times over the years, and it was also near Place Vendôme, where the Ritz Hotel was located.

Actually, I had first visited Harry's years earlier at the suggestion of Gerry Grady, a friend from Endicott, New York. Gerry had spent some years in Europe while in the U.S. Army, and he got to know Harry's owner, Andy McElhone. Andy was the son of the original Scottish partner of Todd Sloan, a famous American jockey. McElhone eventually acquired Harry's from Todd and continued all its best traditions. The establishment was an old and wonderful bar and restaurant frequented by journalists, expats, and many famous people. It was first established in 1911 by Todd Sloan, who bought an actual bar in New York and had it shipped to Paris. Harry's clientele over the years included famous people such as Knute Rockne, Jack Dempsey, Rita Hayworth, Humphrey Bogart, "James Bond," and many others. The piano bar is where George Gershwin reportedly composed "An American in Paris. "

Harry's had many special features. For me, it was the first-class restaurant and the plain, homey, and friendly environment with lots of interesting people. I also got to know Andy MacElhone. One highlight was that Harry's had an old-fashioned hot dog machine sitting on the bar and it had the greatest hot dogs anywhere. Harry's was also where drinks like the Bloody Mary, the Sidecar, the Monkey's Gland, and others were said to have been invented. Visiting Harry's was always the highlight of any trip to Paris for me, and I hope it hasn't changed.

Upstate New York

My early years at IBM included many activities that were not necessarily just IBM or competitive analysis. In the mid-1960s, during my assignment to the IBM Endicott laboratory, I was quite interested in playing ice hockey. We did not have any local artificial ice, so we would drive up to Colgate on the snowy winter road (Route 12B), about an hour away to Hamilton, New York, to rent and play on their rink on Sunday mornings. I got to know the Colgate ice hockey coach, Ron Ryan, during these trips, and one of our discussions turned to the cost of ice hockey sticks. It turned out that this was a major expense for him due to the breakage and variability of the wood sticks that were commonly used at the time.

This struck a responsive chord in me, since I was having the same personal cost exposure myself. The sticks at that time had wood handles, sometimes with an overlay of fiberglass in the wooden blade. I thought that it would be an easy solution for my friends who ran the advanced materials development lab at IBM Endicott, so when I got home I called them up and explained the problem. The lab materials manager at that time was a friend of mine and was interested as well.

His lab had a great deal of the latest materials evaluation equipment for testing, such as an Instron machine, which we could use for evaluation. Our intent was to unofficially develop an application, manufacturing process, and design and structure that IBM would have some ownership in. I spent considerable time in the evenings at IBM, evaluating wood sticks and their costs, and comparing advantages and disadvantages, which were many.

It turned out that at the time, there were no standards at all on ice hockey sticks, other than the maximum allowable blade size 3 x 12 inches, although blades in practice were closer to 2.5 x 10 inches to keep the weight down. The handles were primarily ash and the blades, elm. Players preferred the lightest of sticks, but they had to be stiff and strong in the handle as well as balanced. I began to take wood sticks into the IBM materials lab at night for testing purposes, and tested many wood hockey sticks and determined measurement standards that represented a good stick.

Then came the difficult part—the wood stick handle cross section was a de facto standard that people were used to, so I couldn't change that. This meant that any replacement was required to have the same size handle cross section. In addition, the blade was mainly of wood and was inclined to splinter, absorb water, and break frequently. The handle was a bending stiffness and strength problem, and the blade was an impact and wear problem. All of a sudden, the technical challenges became very large, since any replacement for the handle had to duplicate the wood weight and the blade had to be no higher in weight that the wood.

All the substitute materials were much heavier than wood. Initial substitutes, such as filament-wound handles, did not have the right rectangular-shaped handles, so it became obvious that a replacement handle had to be rectangular and hollow while still being strong and stiff in order to meet the feel and weight challenge as well as the strength objective. At that time, the emergence of graphite prepreg was becoming known, but it was very expensive.

Graphite prepreg is a very strong, lightweight synthetic fiber in an uncured fiber form that contains uncured epoxy to hold it together until it is fired. It is in a class of materials known as advanced composites. Once fired around an object and cured in an oven, it is very strong and tough. At the time, the volumes of this material used for fishing poles and other applications had not yet materialized to drive the cost down. Our initial objective was to get a design and product that had all the required mechanical advantages and could last ten times longer as a wood stick, at five times the cost.

In the process of taking ice hockey sticks through the IBM guard booths into our materials lab center, my boss learned what I was doing. He called me into his office one day and said he would have to fire me, except I had so many people in the IBM materials lab working on the project that they couldn't fire everyone. So I promised not to do any more work using the IBM materials lab people or equipment. I then met with Dr. Ed Cranch, the head of the mechanical engineering department at Cornell University and also an avid hockey player. He agreed to collaborate and enable us to use the architectural testing tables at Cornell for the beam tests.

Eventually, we finished the design and were able to produce prototypes. They consisted of a hollow fiberglass and graphite handle, attached to a large 3 x 12-inch blade with many holes in it to reduce weight, and were made of a high-impact polycarbonate material. However, at that time, we could never get the cost down. It was probably twenty to thirty years later that synthetic ice hockey sticks began incorporating our structure and materials due to the reduced cost of those materials. However, we did get one patent issued for the curved ice hockey stick.

An interesting footnote during the ice hockey stick development venture was my attempt to raise funds to further develop the process and design. My lawyer at the time suggested I talk to one of his clients, who I then met with to describe what I was attempting to do. He in turn suggested that we visit one of his benefactors in the Northeastern Pennsylvania area, so we drove down to that person's business near Clark Summit to present my idea.

As we neared the location, I noticed a large wall that enclosed the property and several guards at the front entrance. Upon entering the building, I was introduced to Russell Buffalino (the Quiet Don). Only years later did I find out he was one of the top leaders of organized crime in the United States and one of the attendees at the Apalachin convention. Of course, I knew nothing about Mr. Buffalino; to me, he seemed very dapper and smart and asked many appropriate business and product-design questions.

When I finished with my presentation, he indicated that he was very interested in investing but that I had to get rid of the current shareholders and that he wanted to have an insurance policy on me in case something happened to me because I was so involved in the project. His suggestion made sense to me, but the project was unable to become cost competitive due to the advanced material cost necessary at the time, so I had little choice but to terminate the project.

While this turned out to be an unsuccessful business venture at the time, I learned a great deal about materials and structures that indirectly benefited me in my competitive analysis job at IBM.

Egypt

On one of my many business and clandestine trips around the world, I had occasion to travel to Egypt. This trip was my first exposure to one of the oldest and most advanced civilizations on the planet. Egyptian history goes back to about 3000 BC (5000 years ago), and it was the most advanced worldwide civilization for many thousands of years. It predated the birth of Mohammed and Islam, in about 650 AD, by about 3000 years.

Egypt's historical achievements in construction and agriculture are legendary. However, radical Islam, by their actions, have proven to be destroyers of the advanced of civilization's artifacts that are of historical, worldwide importance and achievement. I hope that doesn't happen to Egypt's history.

My visits to Karnak, the Valley of the Kings, and Aswan were particularly memorable, as were the monuments at Abu Simbel and, of course, the pyramids. I visited the rose granite quarries in Aswan and noted one obelisk that had been chiseled while still in the ground on its outline. As it happened, when the stone was ready for shipment by boat north toward Cairo on the Nile many miles away, this 110-ton, 100 x 3-foot-long giant stone cracked and so was left in the ground and abandoned where it probably still is today.

Imagine, 4500 years ago, chiseling that out of the ground and removing it, transporting it to the Nile, and then loading it onto a barge in order to float it a long way to its destination to be finished and erected. Even today, with all our modern construction equipment, that would be challenge. The Egyptians had none of our modern equipment and depended on hand labor, ramps, wedges, barges, iron tools, ropes, and the wheel to move everything.

I came away from this trip with a great appreciation for the historical importance and achievements of Egypt. While I was on the way to the airport to leave Egypt, traffic was very heavy. Pedestrians, bicycles, motor bikes, cars, and trucks all shared the roads. My taxi driver unfortunately hit another car, and my driver and the other car's driver both got out and had a fist fight in the road. Fortunately, I was near the airport and was able to carry my bag and get to my flight on time.

CHAPTER 15

Reflections

In thinking about my career and this book, for the benefit of my family and readers I have some thoughts that seem appropriate. I hope you will bear with me as I share them with you. While some passages in this book are highly technical, I have tried to put those into attached reference areas so that the lay reader does not have to read through those unless they so desire.

Having been fortunate enough to travel extensively for over sixty years to Asia, the Middle East, the United States, and Europe, courtesy of the U.S. military and large and successful corporations, I have formed a view of computer technology, past world events, and prospects for the future. Some of the projects I worked on had national value to the United States. As a citizen and patriot, I think it very important for each of us to do what we can to help our country, especially today.

One military project I was involved in during the 1950s was very important to the United States and its partners during the height of the Cold War with Russia. The project was directly under the control of General Nathan Twining; Curtis Lemay, then head of the U.S. Air Force; Allen Dulles, head of the CIA; and John Foster Dulles, who was the U.S. Secretary of State. Dwight Eisenhower was president and directly involved in major project decisions. At the end of this successful project, which preceded the U2 missions, we were awarded the outstanding unit citation for a mission unprecedented in the history of the national military establishment.

While I was at IBM as a senior engineer, I was fortunate to have had exposure at the highest levels within IBM due to my competitive technology analysis work and assignments. This exposure included members of the IBM board of directors, the president of IBM, and heads of major divisions both in the domestic and world trade organizations. In addition, I was privileged to be selected by Nick Katzenbach to be responsible for a project at the CIA where an evaluation and forecast of Soviet/communist technology was required. Later, I was involved in additional confidential projects for the CIA.

After I retired from IBM, I was fortunate to work for other public companies like DuPont, the Dover Corporation, Dover Electronics, and eventually the Dovatron Corporation as vice president of Technology, where I specialized in acquisitions before I retired from that company.

If I were to make any suggestions to my family, friends, and readers, I would only say to live in the real world and not in a vacuum of ignorance and intolerance. Do not overlook real threats, and take timely steps to prevent unforeseen and undesirable circumstance from happening. For surely if time makes those decisions and actions because of your inaction, you may not like the result.

References and Personal Endorsements

T. G. Fisher	12/1/1969	Endorsement
E. H. Goldman	3/8/1970	Endorsement
N. Mii	6/29/1971	Japanese CA Plan Endorsement
R. Rinne	3/21/1972	Endorsement
G. R. Gunther-Mohr	10/25/1971	Endorsement
D. R. Franck R. Avgherinos	1/17/1973	Competitive Analysis I Japan Proposal
J. Keffer	3/6/1971	CA Japan Endorsement
J. Rogers	1/26/1973	Endorsement
R. Immershein	3/12/1970	Endorsement

IBM Executive IBM CA Presentations Personally Made by D. Franck

J. Bertram, et al.	1/4/1973
EPT Staff	1/4/1973
Dr. Gomory	1/9/1973
CTC Committee	1/15/1973
P. Rizzo & staff	1/17/1973
J. Greenman & staff	1/18/1973
N. Katzenbach	1/26/1973
W. Doud	12/01/1972
R. Evans & staff	12/15/1972
P. Fagg & staff	12/21/1972
T. Papes & staff	12/15/1972
R. Sayegh & staff	2/23/1973
J. Rogers & staff	1/30/1973

Executive IBM CA Presentations Made by D. Franck

J. Simek	5/3/1988		
D. Dineinger & staff	2/23/1973		
T. Papes & staff	1/22/1973		
J. Keffer & staff	3/6/1973		
R. Vaughn	11/20/1973		
G. Werbizky	4/29/1974		
R. McFadden	1/30/1974		
B. Ittner	3/21/1974		
Dr. E. Davis	7/29/1974		
J. Mangini	6/21/1974		
E. Brosseau	9/4/1974		
S. Reed	11/14/1974		
M. P. Wahl	11/18/1974	11/27/1974	
F. Moisset	11/22/1974		
J. Keffer	12/27/1974	1/16/1975	6/23/1975
A. Blodgett	12/28/1976		
P. Toole	1/26/1979	7/25/1983	
E. Shapiro	2/21/1979		
E. Boerger	3/22/1979		
C. Conti	10/8/1979	3/18/1980	
J. Kuehler	8/5/1980		
D. Nelson	4/4/1979		
R. Wingart	6/5/1979		
E. Linde	12/2/1980		
D. Gavis	9/18/1974		
E. Davis	7/25/1983		

IBM Competitive Analysis Reports Principally Written by D. Franck

Cob vs. Cocob for Competition	12/1/1966
Competition on Electronic Packaging	12/16/1966
Module on Board	8/24/1966
Packaging Study and Analysis	2/22/1967
Computer Manufacturers/Vendors	3/1/1967
IEEE Commercial Analysis	4/4/1967
Burroughs Illiac IV	5/23/1967
Forecast of Competitive Technology (Farr-McGlaughlin-Patrick)	5/23/1967
Vendor Analysis	7/11/1967
Nepcon East Trade Show	7/11/1967
Minuteman 2 IC Reliability (Lo Hill)	7/20/1967
Westinghouse Elec Multilayer Ceramic Cards	7/24/1967
Semiconductor Memory Products (Reiner)	7/24/1967
ACS Risk	7/28/1967
Honeywell Ceramic Package	7/31/1967
Wescon and 8th International Semiconductor Conference	9/28/1967
ICL Announces Major Addition to 1900 Series	11/1967
Honeywell 88200 Card Analysis	12/18/1967
Motorola Package	12/27/1967
AD Tech LSI Systems (Lo Hill)	1/9/1968
Trip Report to National Technology	2/6/1968
Abstract of Competition – 1968 to 1973	2/8/1968
Nepcon – West Long Beach, Calif.	2/12/1968
Technology Evolution	3/26/1968
Component Industry Report	12/1968
NLT-Planar Package	3/18/1969
Electronic Packaging Trends	4/2/1969
Spring Joint Computer Conference	5/28/1969
Competitive Analysis	9/20/1969
Large Board Shoebox Package	10/31/1969
MSI-LSI ICL1906A Printed Circuit Manuf. and Design	11/25/1969

IBM Competitive Analysis Reports Principally Written by D. Franck

UK Commercial Analysis	11/25/1969
Commercial Packaging Analysis – British Technology	12/1/1969
Fall Joint Computer Conference – Las Vegas	12/29/1969
Discussion for Outlook of Minis (Zimbel)	1/1970
Small Machine Design	1/2/1970
System Statistics – Component Report (Rizzi)	1/5/1970
Vendor Purchases	3/16/1970
Verbal CA Presentation – Las Vegas	3/16/1990
Nepcon West	3/18/1970
CDC Experimental System (Reiner)	3/31/1970
CDC Large Scale Experimental System (Reiner)	3/31/1970
CA Packaging Summary Division Report	4/21/1970
IEEE Conference	4/2/1970
Nepcon West Conference	4/23/1970
Miniware Study	5/13/1970
Industry Minicomputers (Beckman)	5/25/1970
Vendor Supplement Report	6/3/1970
CDC (Beckman)	6/5/1970
Modular Processing Systems Report	6/15/1970
Trip Reports:	
Photocircuits	4/23/1970
Hannover Fair/Germany	5/3/1970
Spring Joint Comp Conference	5/7/1970
WTC German CA Presentation	5/4/1970
Electronic Industry Trends (purchased)	7/25/1970
Minicomputers and the Arts (Beckman)	7/28/1970
Nepcon East	8/7/1970
CA Electronic Packaging Presentations	8/21/1970
Multiwire (Hill)	8/27/1970
Illiac Boards (Rinne)	9/21/1970
Multiwire (Lester)	9/2/1970

IBM Competitive Analysis Reports Principally Written by D. Franck

Competitive Electronic Packaging	9/8/1970
Burroughs Illiac Boards (Rinne)	9/1/1970
Photocircuit Multiwire	9/9/1970
Wescon LA	9/10/1970
Burroughs Illiac IV Boards	9/22/1970
CDC 7600 Versus the 370/195	9/23/1970
Augat Visit	10/1/1970
Photocircuits Multiwire	10/2/1970
Inforex and Multiwire	10/7/1970
Competitive Status Cabling and Wiring	10/8/1970
RCA Claims and 370 Comparison (Mangini)	10/9/1970
Cost Estimate Illiac IV Boards (Asher)	10/12/1970
RCA Evaluations (Slade)	10/12/1970
Illiac IV Card Costs	10/23/1970
Inforex-Infobond (Rinne)	10/23/1970
CA Budget	10/28/1970
Inforex (Meany)	10/27/1970
BEMA Show	11/2/1970
Nerem Conference	11/6/1970
Fall Joint Computer Conference	11/16/1970
Bunker Ramo Electronic Packaging	11/23/1970
Metal Board	12/7/1970
Bunker Ramo BR1018 Planar Coax	1971
Competitive Analysis Report	1/20/1971
Computer Designers' Conference (Haiber)	1/25/1971
NCR 50/NCR100 Packaging	1/28/71 & 2/1/71
Nepcon West	2/9/1971
Components Division CA for Pkg. Strategy	3/22/1971
Spring Joint Computer Conference	5/17/1971
Nepcon East (DePaolo)	7/11/1971
Nepcon East	6/15/1971

IBM Competitive Analysis Reports Principally
Written by D. Franck

First Level Competitive Pkg. Data	7/29/1971
Analysis of Texas Inst Keyboard (Scmerer)	8/2/1971
Wescon	10/7/1971
TI Edgemount Conn.	9/1/1971
System 370 Partitioning in MPT (Minnich)	7/8/1971
Competition Packaging Status	9/29/1971
Wescon	10/7/1971
Multilayer Ceramic Competition	10/20/1971
Multi-chip Module Competition	10/21/1971
Annual CA Report (1969–1976)	10/27/1971
Nerem Convention	11/25/1971
Fall Joint Computer Conference – Las Vegas	11/17/1971
Components Division Measurements	12/7/1971
Four Phase Computer System	1/13/1972
General Instrument 2048 Ram (Gajda)	2/19/1972
Nepcon West & Semiconductor ICs	2/10/1972
Vendor Reports (Gajda)	2/14/1972
Motorola Trip Report – Phoenix (Stettinius)	2/15/1972
Texas Instruments Trip Report (Stettinius)	2/16/1972
Fairchild Trip Report (Glembocki)	3/2/1972
Raytheon Trip Report (Campbell)	3/2/1972
Inteersil Trip Report (Stettinius)	3/1972
Advanced Micro Trip Report (Glembocki)	3/6/1972
IEEE Convention	3/1972
Memory Competitive Packaging	4/4/1972
Competitive Substrate Costs	4/4/1972
Fairchild Visit	4/5/1972
Report on Printed Circuit Domestic Sourcing (Lausi)	4/14/1972
Minneapolis Honeywell	4/26/1972
CA Information for Hermann for Japan Visit (Moyer)	5/2/1972
American Lava Trip Report	5/5/1972

DON FRANCK

IBM Competitive Analysis Reports Principally Written by D. Franck

Metceram Trip Report	5/8/1972
First and Second Level CA 1971–1976	5/12/1972
Electronic Components Conference – Washington, D.C.	5/15/1972
Spring Joint Computer Conference – Atlantic City	5/16/1972
Future Honeywell Design Considerations (Lo Hill)	5/24/1972
Vendor Costs for MLC	6/12/1972
Nepcon East	6/13/1972
Hitachi Screened MLC/SMC and Auto Fab	6/19/1972
AADC Module	6/26/1972
MCM/MLC Competitive Activities	7/25/1972
MCM vs. SCM	8/3/1972
Bell Labs 1A Computer	8/4/1972
Vendor MLC Prices	11/28/1972
Competitive Wafer Packaging	12/13/1972
Competitive Packaging Report, 1971–1980, First and Second Level	1/19/1973
Japanese Competitive Systems (Avgherinos and Franck)	3/19/1973
Institute of Printed Circuits Meeting	4/12/1973
Test Equipment Marketing Study	4/13/1973
Electronic Components Conference Notes (Miller)	5/16/1973
National Computer Conference (Clarke)	6/20/1973
Second Level CA Assessment	9/21/1973
Nova Computer Series Status	1/2/1974
Competitive Input for the SPD Technical Strategy	1/11/1974
Nova Type Packaging	1/29/1974
Nepcon West – Anaheim	2/1974
International Solid State Circuits Conference - Philadelphia	3/4/1974
GE/Toshiba Manufacturing Process	3/12/1974
FS Competitiveness	3/22/1974
Competitive Technology Report 1973–1978	4/3/1974
IEEE Packaging Workshop (Miller)	5/30/1974
Digital Equipment Report	6/26/1974

IBM Competitive Analysis Reports Principally Written by D. Franck

Wafer Technology	7/2/74 & 8/6/74
I/O COB Competitive Position for the 3270 (Harrison and Franck)	8/22/1974
Competitive Assessment – Testers	8/26/1974
VTL vs. MST at the Box Level	9/12/1974
Wescon Conference (Harrison)	9/24/1974
Projected SS/IO Capability	12/31/1974
Chip Technology to System Overview	12/31/1974
F100K Fairchild Sub Nano Second ECL (Muller/Owens)	2/3/1975
SPD/GSD Competitive Position (Franck/Hellwarth)	2/12/1975
Competitive Summary (1977-1980)	3/12/1975
STS Competitive Status	3/17/1975
Cost Performance Trends	4/17/1975
SPD Measurement and Competitive Operations	4/28/1975
Algorex Study	5/6/1974
Interdata Study	5/28/1975
Tape Technology and Chip Carriers	6/9/1975
SS/I/O Competitive Analysis	6/15/1975
Large System Competitive Estimate	7/11/1975
Hitachi M Series Competitive Assessment	8/22/1975
Competitive Technology	8/22/1975
Packaging Flash SPD Competition	2/22/1976
Competitive Packaging Technology	4/13/1976
Nepcon Canada	5/18/1976
Low End Competitive Environment	5/18/1976
NCC and IEEE (Simmons/Franck)	6/13/1979
Packaging in Japan (Fujisawa Dev Lab)	9/1980
Packaging in Japan (Fujisawa Dev Lab)	9/1981
Summary Status of JCMs	10/20/1981
M Series Technology Summary (Fujisawa Dev Lab)	12/1975
Interrelationships Computers and Japanese Government	1983

IBM Competitive Analysis Reports Principally
Written by D. Franck

Performance of Various Computers (Dongarra-Argonne Lab)	7/1984
Frey Report on MITI (Frey)	5/1985
Fifth Generation JCM Computer Systems (RIS)	9/30/1985
Japan's Super Smart Computer Project (Asian WSJ)	9/30/1985
PCB Comparisons, Japan vs. IBM	12/13/1985
System Perf and Tech Trends (Franck/Kellerman)	5/1985

The history of reports I have attached is not entirely complete. Over the years I had continuous contact and exposure to local and senior IBM executives within IBM regarding competitive analysis.

APPENDIX 1

Technical Detail: Chapter 7: Japanese Competitive Analysis Technology Training Program and Development of a Formal CA Group

The resources available at IBM during the early 1970s were the following:

Location	Area	# of People	Years in Op
Fishkill, NY	Logic	~6-8	~6
Burlington, VT	Memory	~3	1
Endicott, NY	Packaging	1	~6
Harrison, NY	Staff	1	1

In order to put an effective worldwide CA group in place, we needed the following training and personnel:

Task	Management Training	Technologist Training
Review of CA Mission and Organization	3 days	3 days
Review of Data Collection Sources and Methods	1 week	2 weeks
Data Bank Methods	3 days	2 weeks

General Familiarization with Files and Technology

Task	Management Training	Technologist Training
Packaging Technology	1 week	3 weeks

- Small System and Input-Output Equipment
- High-Performance Computers
- Cost-Performance Computers
- First Level – Chip and Module Level
- Second Level – Printed Circuit or Card Level

Task	Management Training	Technologist Training
Logic Device/Function Technology	1 day	1 week
Memory Device/ Basic System Memory Technology	2 days	1 week

Training Program (Develop working knowledge – see attached)

	3 weeks	3 months
		1.5 years
Total Time	~ 7 weeks	~ 21–70 weeks

APPENDIX 2

Technical Detail: Chapter 10: IBM Analysis of the Russian Computer Technology for the CIA

Some Observations from Data Review, 1976–1979

Many Western countries solicited to make proposals for establishing printed circuit factories. CII highlighted (France):

- Chronic Soviet communist problems

- Labor basically inefficient and nonproductive

- Low yields for common and simple parts

- Poor volume/less than equipment capable of

- Water supply and pressure variable and unreliable

- Power shortages and interruptions common

- Purchase of turnkey factories that do not work as per their needs due to their own problems

- Ground pollution and complaints due to PC chemical spillage and sewage

- While U.S. and French semiconductor chips were okay, their own chips caused cooling problems

Projections for Western World

20 mil lines – 1960s

14 mil lines – 1970s or PCBs

8 mil lines – Early 1980s

4 mil lines – Mid 1980s

- The Soviet equivalents are about factor of 1.5 to 2 worse than projected technical norms cited above for printed circuit technology.

- Showed flexible circuit interest at Inter-Nepcon 1978, requiring 15 mil lines.

- Hitachi and Fujitsu were asked in 1978 to bid on/set up a PC factory. Rejected due to Coordinating Committee for Multilateral Export Controls, which placed controls on exports to communist counties' commitments.

- Bought fifty automatic drilling machines from the United States in 1978, and in 1977 bought thirty-three Retab 4000 Swedish machines.

- Thompson CSF, Paris, was to sell a dry film plant to Soviets.

All Quotes for PC Factories Had Complexities at the Following Levels, 1977–1980

12 mil lines ≤ 3:1 aspect ratio

Mostly 2-sided, some multilayer (14 layers)

1 LPC (wanted 2 LPC, but "realized it couldn't be done easily")

- Wire wrap, predominantly by hand tools.

- Back panels are typically wire wrap with twisted pair on newer requirements.

- Gold usage very tightly restricted and statements made as to disapproval of its use. If this were true on PC connectors and card tab areas for mainframe computers, there would have been a severe reliability effect. However, in other areas they exhibited great concern for system down time and reliability.

- Good theoretical understanding of packaging leverages, tradeoffs, and electrical requirements (i.e., triplate and strip line analysis, noise, density, power distribution, cooling, etc., as it affects system performance).

- One pictorial display showed an interstitial VIA.

- Connector densities typically on 0.100" centers (or less dense).

- TTL used in RYAD I, and ECL in RYAD II, although they had considerable problems with cooling the ECL initially (DIPS used entirely).

- DIP modules (plastic and ceramic) commonly used. Logic circuit densities 15 to 30 gates chip/module today and 5 to 15 gates mid-1970s (must be de-rated to get circuits). They also used RC packs in DIP form factors.

- Flat cables commonly used—mostly wire wrap for other connections.

- Volume and reliability were very likely of much less capability than Western computer manufacturers, even when the Soviets were able to manufacture a machine at equivalent performance.

- ERLORG was a worldwide marketing distributor of component technology and was a good source of where and how their components were used in real application (i.e., RYAD I and RYAD II).

- The Unified Electronic Computer System encompasses the entire development organization and all countries and assignments (ESEUM).

- The excessive number of card layers did not coincide with the component density, even considering 1 Line Per Channel (LPC) technology. It is possible that their automatic wiring algorithms were very inefficient or subject to long machine running times, or the hand layouts were very poor.

- Severe differences of claim on several parameters.

- Performance of machine can vary by 50 percent.

- Circuit performance claimed = 10 NS one time, 15 NS another.

- TEZ is "typical replacement element," (i.e., FRU).

- "Trend is toward IC (SCM), not MCM or Hybrid" (their claim). I believe they expected to push chip integration and not go hybrid (or MCM) to get improved performance for the next five to ten years. Hitachi and Fujitsu also used SCMs in HP machines.

- Council on the use of computer hardware (SPSUT) was for coordination and planning.

- Series 500 ESL is ECL 10K equivalent. It is used in RYAD II in a 60- to 70-OHM impedance environment.

- A common maintenance complaint concerned misaligned contacts on cards/board and faulty power supply blocks and poor connector/cables.

- India was a common source for hardware and information on IBM in the Soviet Union.

- The small system and input/output product cards were used in RYAD I and II were much simpler than the CPU cards.

- Reference was made to IBM documents.

- Cards had an overcoat for protection.

At the time, the available Soviet database of information on important technology and performance parameters was seriously weak, of limited quantity, and sometimes of doubtful accuracy as compared to our own Western computer database. Therefore, the judgments and accuracy of prediction were of concern. However, it was believed the data could be obtained relatively easily over a reasonable period of time from public data, sources, and observations.

It should also be noted that even the Western technical data from IBM or Japan were often based on judgment and averages or "typicals," rather than an absolute exact number, but at least it was relatively complete.

For representation purposes, the machines selected for Soviet RYAD I were primarily based on an assumption that their 2030 CPU at 0.100 MIPS shipped in June, 1974 was a cost/performance (C/P) CPU, and that the RYAD II 2055 CPU (FCS 79) with 0.8 MIPS was one of its C/P follow-on computers. There were apparently intermediate CPUs using an advanced form of RYAD I technology, such as the 2032 and 2033, that could also be classed as cost/performance machines with an FCS of 1975 and 1976.

For high-performance (HP) class CPUs, the RYAD I-2050 and I-2040 CPUs, with performances of 0.5 MIPS and 0.3 MIPS respectively, were selected with FCS dates of 1974 to 1976. The follow-on HP CPUs used in RYAD II were the 2060 and 2065 machines with FCS dates between 1979 and 1982. These latter machines had performances of 1.5 MIPS and 4.5 MIPS respectively. In general, "cost" is a relatively precise value in Western understanding. There is no basis for an equivalent cost for the RYAD hardware in this paper, and so the appointment to certain RYAD machines to either the cost or high performance machines is highly subjective.

High-Performance CPU Summary

	1974–1976	1979–1980	1982	1990
Russian Years Behind –Performance	11	8	5–6	3
Russian Years Behind – Technology	4.9	6.1	7.1	7.8
Russian Effective CPU Years Behind	11	8	7.1	7.8
Major Cause of Negative Status	Primarily system design	Primarily system design	Better balance but technology limited	Primarily technology limited

Conclusions – Soviet Union Status:

7. They will have to build high-performance system out of primitive technology or acquire technology or CPUs for future products/usage.

8. There is probably a serious negative reliability effect upon system downtime, if using older technology.

9. The multiprocessor versions of older hardware will have better performance than uniprocessors. Special high-performance array processors can be built out of primitive technology.

10. Ability to manufacture and service in quantity is believed much less than West.

11. Logic and packaging technology was seriously weak; memory probably is as well.

12. There is a serious and difficult technology hurdle in bridging from 4.5 MIP uniprocessors to 40-MIP machine forecast for 1990, with incremental performance machines required along the way.

Cost-Performance CPU Summary

	1974–1976	1979–1980	1982	1990
Russian Years Behind –Performance	5–6	3–4	2–3	3
Russian Years Behind – Technology	4.9	4	2.8	3.1
Russian Effective CPU Years Behind	5–6	3–4	2–3	3.1
Major Cause of Negative Status	Primarily system design	Primarily system design	Mix of technology and system design	Primarily technology

Conclusions – Soviet Union Status:

* Cost-performance machines were much easier to attain with primitive technology than high-performance machines.

* Technology through 1982 was adequate to obtain CPU/CP goals somewhat later than West. Growth in performance to 12 MIPS in 1990 would require some new technology extensives to be developed.

* MP versions of existing hardware can meet CPU performance objectives. Special processors (array and F-point) would help CPU performance—special job streams.

* Ability to manufacture and service in quantity was believed much less than West.

* Some derating of the effect of the technology lack was made due to the lesser need for technology in this performance class (1979 to 1990).

	1974–1976	1979–1980	1982	1990
Logic Chip Design	7	8	9	10
Logic Chip I/Os	5	5.5	6	6
Logic Ckt. Delay-1	3	4	4.5	6.5
Logic Ckt. Delay-2	3.5	3	3.5	3
FRU I/O Grid	-0-	4	7	8
Ckt. Power ECL	3.5	6	6	7
Photolithology (ucrons)	13	10	10	10
Module I/Os	6	8	9.5	12
FRU Ckts.	3	5	6	9
FRU I/Os	3	5	6	6.5
Printed Circuit Complexity*	6.5	9	11	16
	4.9	6.1	7.1	7.8

Note: Ckt. Delay and Ckt. Power mix ECL and TTL, and as such, are useful as a general indicator but are not specific.

* LPC x Layers / Grid x LW

Parameter Description

On a separate report, I had detailed the many descriptions of parameters that are considered first-order indicators of technology or system performance levels. It is important that those parameters be used only once, for a vintage of technology. For instance, although the IBM SLT-1965 technology was used for a wide range of CP and HP machines through 1970, it can only be used once on a curve when it was first shipped to a customer in a product. Subsequent models would not also be plotted as far as technology is concerned.

When a new technology is introduced, its first use is then plotted, as for example the IBM Monolithic Semiconductor Technology 1971 technology. In this way, a curve is created of FCS dates as related to new technology introductions. For machine performance and cycle time, a breakdown of cost performance and high performance has been done. For technology, the CP/HP measurements have been combined since the differences are not large when taken as a group and lumped under "mainframe CPU" data. I have selected some examples of the Russian RYAD Series as compared to the rest of the non-Russian world.

Basic Soviet Technology Assumptions for CPUs

Please note that these data were the best judgment of the source data provided. There are many missing parameters that are very important, for which no data was available or provided. An analysis of the Western data and projections will show the missing and additional data desired.

Machines Selected	RYAD I			RYAD II		
	2030	2040	2050	2055	2060	2065
FCS	6-74	6-74	6-76	6-79	6-79	6-82
MIPS	0.1	0.380	0.500	0.800	1.5	4.5
Cycle Time (NS)				125	60	
Chip Circuits/Module	3	3	3	8	8	20
Chip I/Os/Module	16	16	16	16–24	16–24	16–28
Ckt. Delay/Unloaded Ckt.	10	10	3.0	2.0	2.0	1.5
Ckt. Power (Avg.)	10	10	25	25	25	20
(FRU) Card Size (inch)	5.5x9.3	5.5x9.3	5.5x9.3	6.5x5.7	6.5x5.7	6x11
Card ICs	72	72	72	60	60	60
Card Circuits (FRU)	216	216	216	480	480	1200
Card I/Os	96	96	96	135	135	270
Card I/O Grid	0.100	0.100	0.100	0.100	0.100	0.100
Card Layers	7–9	7–9	7–9	8–10	8–10	8–12
Card LPC	1	1	1	1	1	1
Card Hole Grid	0.100	0.100	0.100	0.100	0.100	0.1
Card Line Width (Mils)	12	12	12	10	10	10
Photo Lithography	15	15	10	9	9	6
PC Complexity*	7.5	7.5	7.5	10	10	12

* LPC x Layers / Grid x LW

High-Performance MIPS

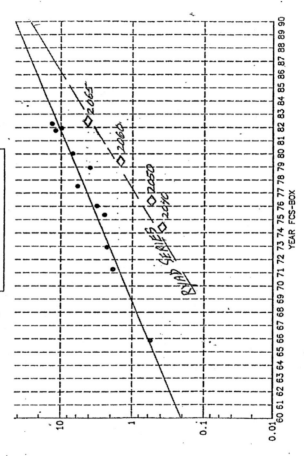

Mainframe CPUs – Semiconductor Chip Circuits

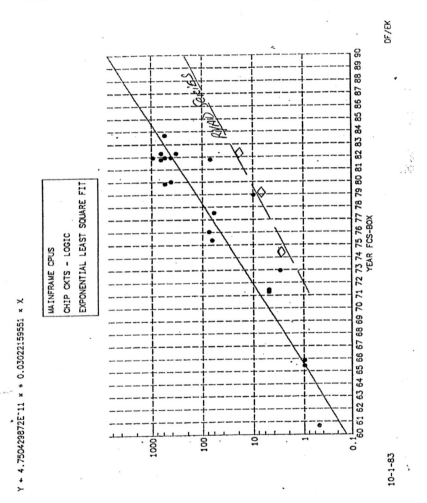

$Y + 4.750429872E^{-}11 \times * 0.03022159551 \times X$

Mainframe CPUs – Power/Circuit

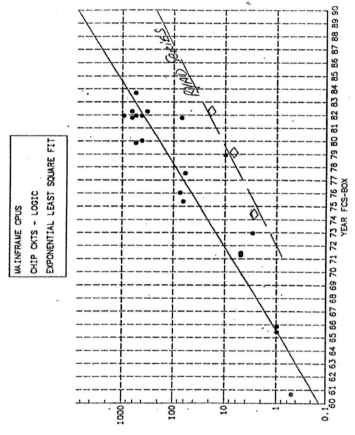